MACHINES OF THE DEAD 3

DAVID BERNSTEIN

SEVERED PRESS
HOBART TASMANIA

MACHINES OF THE DEAD 3

CHAPTER 1

Maria pinned the snowmobile's throttle to the handlebar grip and raced up the highway. Zaun was holding on tight, squeezing her abdomen and making it difficult for her to breathe.

Someone was shooting at them.

Jill was dead.

Jack had been shot.

Everything had been going so smoothly, and then in seconds everything was going terribly wrong.

She'd been on the battlefield, performed dangerous and covert operations, and been involved in gunfights where she was pinned down and under heavy fire. But it had never become easy to deal with. There was no getting used to life-threatening situations.

Staring ahead, all she concentrated on was reaching the overpass. A ramp veered off to the right—the Galleria Mall's exit—and traveled around and over the highway.

Moving at such a speed, Maria knew it would be difficult for the shooter to hit her or Zaun, but not impossible. Based on how Jack and Jill had been shot, she knew the shooter was a damn good shot and was somewhere off to the right, positioned on the hill. Having glanced over a few times, she'd seen a strip mall about 200 feet away. There were no other structures in the area— only open terrain and thick woods behind them.

Of course, there could be more than one shooter, but she didn't think so. Single shots had been taken. They were spaced apart— measured and deliberate.

The snowmobile dipped and Maria had the breath expelled from her lungs as Zaun squeezed harder. He was yelling something to her, but the roar of the engine and the whipping of wind made his words indecipherable. She only hoped he'd be able to hold on until they reached safety.

A minute later, they made it to the overpass. The sled zoomed right under and passed it. But she'd gotten them out of the sniper's sights. The overpass was a large blockade ensuring them plenty of room to maneuver safely. She turned the snowmobile around and headed back under the overpass and killed the engine.

"We have to get Jack," Zaun said.

Maria hopped off the sled. "We'll be dead before we get off the sled to grab him," she said, and pulled the Browning 300 from the back of the vehicle. She pointed it back down the snow-covered highway and peered through the scope. Jack was alive. She watched as he shot a few undead. There were a number of bot-controlled corpses in the area and more coming from the mall-side. A few were crouched around Jill's corpse, tearing it to pieces. Good, she thought. That should buy Jack some time.

Maria may not have liked the girl, but she hadn't deserved to go out the way she did.

"We have to do something," Zaun pressed, removing his helmet.

"Jack's okay for now," she lied, hoping to calm Zaun down. She needed him focused. He was injured and there wasn't much he could do but hobble around. "I'm going to check if I can see the shooter. Wait here."

Maria crept to the edge of the overpass wall. There was an incline of snow-covered earth that impaired her view. Moving farther out could prove deadly.

She turned around, headed to the other end of the overpass and climbed up the bank of snow to the road overhead. She crawled, staying low to the guardrail. Higher up, she had a better view of the strip mall while remaining hidden. Peering through her rifle's scope, she scanned the roof of the building and nearly lost her breath at seeing Cable.

Maria's surprise quickly turned to rage. She'd been there when they had a chance to kill him after Zaun bested him in hand-to-hand combat. She could take a chance and try a shot, but at her current distance, along with the gun most likely not calibrated as well as it could be, she'd probably miss. His body was partially blocked by something too. The best tool in her arsenal right now was the element of surprise.

Maria crawled backward and slid down the hill.

Zaun was still sitting on the sled.

"It's Cable," she said.

"What . . ." Zaun smacked the seat. "Damn. I should've killed that son of a bitch. I never thought we'd see him again."

"Yeah, well, we won't make that mistake again."

"See anyone else?"

"No, but that doesn't mean he's alone."

"So what's the plan?"

Normally, Maria would want to scout the area and make sure Cable was unaccompanied. Decide the best course of action. But time was of the essence. Jack was injured, probably dying, or would be dead soon if they didn't get him out of there.

"I'm going to sneak over to the building and kill him along with anyone else in my way," Maria said."

"*We're* going over to that building," Zaun said, correcting her.

Maria shook her head. "You're injured. *We* don't need you opening that wound. And besides, you'll only slow me down and get yourself shot."

Zaun climbed off the sled and stood. "I'm going."

Maria shoved him, and Zaun tumbled backward to the ground.

"What the hell?" he said, wincing in pain. "Are you crazy?"

"I'm making a point. I know you want to help, and you can, but not by coming with me. Did you see how easily I knocked you down?"

She held out a hand and helped him up.

"I get it," he said, "but I can still help."

"Don't make me knock your ass out," Maria threatened.

"I can't just sit here when Jack's life is in danger, and you're going out there against who knows how many people, including Cable. He's not just a psycho, but a well-trained psycho."

Maria shoved the Browning into Zaun's arms. "You're going to cover me and keep Jack safe, and you're going to do it all from here." Zaun was no marksman, but more than capable of helping out.

Maria pointed to where the snow-covered incline met the cement wall of the overpass. "Creep out a little farther than there. You'll be out of Cable's view. Keep an eye on Jack. Take out any zombies that get near him if he passes out."

"What about you?"

"I'll be fine," Maria said. "If Jack seems okay, check on me once in a while." She smiled and winked. "Just stay out of view of the strip mall. Cable's going to know we're here. He knows we won't leave Jack."

Zaun stared at the weapon in his hands, looking perplexed.

"Zaun?" Maria asked.

"Yeah?"

"Are you with me?"

"Yeah," he said, nodding. "Of course. It's just so screwed up. This all happened so fast."

"I need you. Jack needs you."

Maria went over to the snowmobile and removed her M4 rifle. She slung it over her shoulder and then placed two extra magazines for the weapon in her pockets. With her Glock 21 strapped to her hip, she was ready to go.

"Stay safe, and don't try to be a hero," she told Zaun. "I'll be back soon."

Maria left the underpass from the backside. She trudged through the snow across the open field, still below the exit ramp's height. The snow was deep in places, making her work. Sweat quickly built up along her skin—not all of it from exertion.

She was out in the open now; exposed like a wart along smooth flesh. The few trees that dotted the open terrain served as waypoints for her to catch her breath and feel somewhat safe. Keeping an eye on the building—only able to see a view of the side now—she hadn't seen any movement since leaving the overpass.

Pushing on, she made it to a guardrail just short of the woods beyond, realizing she'd run into another road. Leaping over the steel barricade, she hurried across the snow-covered street and into the forest. She doubted anyone from the strip mall would be able to make out her tracks, but it did little to make her feel better.

She worked her way through the woods, staying far enough from the tree line so she couldn't be spotted. Many of the trees were bare leaving only the evergreens as cover. She hadn't heard a gunshot since Jack had fired his weapon. Whether that was a good thing, she did not know. The lack of any shooting meant Cable wasn't using his weapon. No one else had died. Unless Jack *was* dead, hence the reason he wasn't firing his weapon. Or maybe there simply weren't any undead near him yet.

Regardless, Maria couldn't worry about any of that now. She needed to stay on mission using getting back to her daughter and saving her friends as the ultimate motivators.

As she made her way to the tree line, she was grateful it wasn't snowing, wanting a clear line of sight. But the wind was picking up, and the gusts were biting and chilling her sweat-lined body. She tightened the strings on her coat, helping to seal off the cold. Jack could be dying. She didn't want to think like that, but it was the truth. Taking a few deep breaths, pumping herself up, she unslung the M4, and bolted from the skeletal forest.

She reached the guardrail, vaulting it with ease, then ran down the road and up the entrance to the strip mall. Like in a dream, she worked hard but moved slow, the deep snow like mud. Her eyes watered from the wind. She was an easy target for Cable or anyone else he had with him. If a gunman had her in his sights, she was dead. But through teary eyes, she pushed on and scanned the back of the building. All the windows were intact, so she listened for the sound of glass being smashed out, and kept a keen eye on the roof where a sniper would most likely be.

When she made it to the building, she bent over and sucked in much needed air. Her chest heaved, and the cold air made her cough. Then the echo of gunshots sounded, chilling her more than the wicked winter weather. They were coming from around the building in the front. She knew it was Jack, the shots not from a rifle but a handgun. She smiled. Jack was still alive.

She inhaled a lungful of frigid air, slung the M4 over her shoulder and pulled out her sidearm. She unzipped her jacket and slid it off, then pulled off her flannel shirt and t-shirt. She rubbed a few handfuls of snow over her skin to remove the sweat. The cold was heart-stopping and caused her teeth to chatter, but the action was necessary. She needed the sweat gone, knowing it could kill her if hypothermia set in.

Finished, she quickly re-dressed and hugged herself, trying to warm up.

She inched to the corner of the building and peered around it. Seeing the way was clear, she hurried along the wall and came to a door about midway to the front. It was locked. She moved on to the front of the building and was able to see the overpass but not Zaun. Good, he was staying hidden.

Jack and the damaged snowmobile were about 200 feet away. Bodies were scattered around him—the undead that Jack had put down. A quick count showed there were ten undead heading his way with most coming from the Galleria's parking lot and the adjacent woods. There had been a lot of noise earlier, and Jack's continued firing would only attract more of the bot-controlled things. As long as he was conscious, he should have enough ammo to keep them at bay, unless of course a number too great came along. This would be a terrible time for a herd.

There had been a lot of blood loss, and Jack's energy would be drained. Jill's corpse would only last so long before the undead wanted newer meat. She had to get this over with quickly.

Maria poked her head out from around the corner of the building and came face to face with a zombie. Its putrid odor of rot and death hit her like an invisible wave. She staggered backward. The thing's face was intact and appeared fresh, but the eyes had been burned out. Regardless of its blindness, it reached for her.

Ready to shoot, Maria thought better, and withdrew her hunting knife. She needed to be as silent as possible. She led the thing to the side of the building before stabbing it in the temple, ending its unnatural life. It stutter-stepped, then collapsed to the ground.

After wiping off the gore from the blade, she sheathed the weapon and proceeded around the corner to the front of the building. The storefronts were all glass, granting anyone inside a fine view of the outside. The first tenant was an insurance office. She tried the door and found it locked. She could have easily shot out the glass and made her way inside. But again, the noise would alert Cable to her presence.

She moved on to the next door, but it too was locked.

Coming to the halfway point of the building, she found a solid door that led to the second level where other businesses were located. Pulling on the handle, the door opened. A stairwell shrouded in gloom, save for light coming from behind her and a small window above, awaited.

Sidearm in hand, she slowly ascended the staircase and made it to the top without trouble. Opening another door, she found a hallway leading to the right and left, overhead skylights illuminating the way. She took a moment and listened. The place was as silent as a graveyard at midnight.

After giving her eyes a moment to adjust to the lower level of light, she went left, and passed by two offices with the doors closed before coming to one with the door wide open. Peering inside, she saw chairs around a coffee table littered with magazines. A reception counter was located along the back wall. She expected to see ceiling tiles hanging, chairs overturned, and everything in disarray. But things were normal-looking, as if no one had entered the area since the undead arrived. For a moment, she wanted to sit down and pretend she was somewhere else, simply waiting for an appointment. Something normal. Maybe a checkup for her daughter. She looked down at her right hand, the hand that would normally be holding her small child's hand if they had come in for a doctor's appointment. Her heart wrenched.

Maria shook her head and was back to reality, though the pain of not being with her daughter was still present. As much as she hated to do it, she had to put the memories of her child on the backburner. She needed to be focused on doing the job, on killing the enemy. On saving Jack.

Maria backed out of the room and closed the door.

The next office was empty save for indentations in the carpet where chairs and other office furniture had been. She wondered if the business had moved or failed. But none of that mattered, for every business was now gone.

After quietly closing the door, she headed down the hallway and passed by a number of closed doors. If Cable or anyone else was behind one of them, she doubted they'd hear her. Going room to room would come later. Her sights were set on the emergency door at the end of the hall.

Approaching it, she tried peering through the small rectangular window, but it was too dark on the other side to see anything but her reflection in the glass. She pushed on the red handle—the words ALARM WILL SOUND painted on the steel bar—and half expected to hear the rapid ringing of a bell or siren, but knew there would be no sound. It opened a few inches before she stopped and listened.

Damn, she hated moving so slow. She wanted to tear through the place like a whirlwind, kill Cable and let the building crumble over his dead body. But if she wasn't cautious, she'd wind up dead. If she died, Jack died. There was a gunman about, and not just any would-be shooter, but a trained military man. And he might have companions. She figured she had been seen approaching the building, and allowed entrance, only to be taken out inside. Why? She did not know. Then again, she might've caught the bastard off guard. He could still be on the roof looking for her and Zaun and leaving Jack as bait. She wondered how she knew they'd be traveling this way and came to the realization that he hadn't. He had been waiting for anyone to pick off; not them in particular.

Opening the door so she could fit through, Maria slipped into the gloom. It was pitch black. Feeling around, she inched forward and came into contact with a steel banister and stairs. With her Glock at the ready, she headed up to what she guessed would be the roof.

Her blind trek was short.

She came to a landing. A thin beam of light shone ahead along the bottom of a door—a door that she knew led to the roof. Her pulse quickened.

Approaching the door, she pushed on the handle. It opened easily, a cold blast of arctic air rushing over her. The dramatic change of light made her squint. She waited a few moments for her eyes to adjust against the glare, the snow-covered roof multiplying the sun's rays.

She saw boot prints leading to the door, but the cement landing was dry. She wondered if the shooter had heard her and decided to backtrack—keep her from knowing where he had gone.

Backing up a step and moving to the left, she checked to see if someone was waiting for her just outside the doorway. Seeing no one, she stepped forward, staying inside the building, and surveyed as much of the rooftop as possible. Footprints dotted the snow and led in numerous directions. About midway across, there was a grouping of air-conditioning units. At the far end of the roof was another door and small shack-like structure. It was the roof access for the other side of the building. The shooter could have known she was coming up this side and escaped out the other. Or he was coming around, hoping to get the drop on her.

Maria glanced up into the darkness, imagining that the shooter was on top of the access roof, waiting above her like a panther ready to pounce. She'd hoped to get the element of surprise, but it looked like the tables had turned.

Deciding to take a chance, she backed out of the doorway and kept her Glock aimed up at the roof's ledge. As soon the man showed himself, she'd put a few rounds into him. She could quickly turn the disadvantage of her situation back to her advantage.

When she was six feet out, she was able to see enough of the roof and that no one was on it.

Boot prints went around to the sides of the roof access structure.

Stepping back to the doorway, she moved to her right and kept her back to the wall. When she reached the corner, she checked around it, and was relieved to find no one waiting and the snow undisturbed. She did the same for the other side, but this time found footprints leading to the edge of the roof. She followed them and peered over the side, and it all became very clear what had happened. A nylon rope dangled from the roof access structure to the ground. Footprints led from where the rope ended to the front of the building, mixing with hers. When she had walked that way earlier there had been no rope or footprints. The shooter had climbed down the rope when she entered the building.

He was following her. Planning on sneaking up from behind, and what—shoot her in the back? Slit her throat? Shove her off the roof?

Maria froze at hearing the crunch of snow.

A door slammed.

She spun around and saw two zombies come around the corner of the roof access structure. She shot each one in the head, splattering their brains across the snow, and then rushed to the roof exit door, and saw that it was closed. She grabbed the handle, but the door wouldn't open. Whoever was stalking her was having fun. Playing a game. He'd sent two undead after her, but why? He had to know she would easily take them out. Maybe he was hoping to get her to use all her ammo. He could have simply crept up behind her and blown her off the roof. In order to get the undead to the roof, the shooter would have had to manhandle them. That meant taking a chance with his safety. And for what, to screw with her?

She let loose an audible breath, feeling the pressure of the situation pressing down on her. She couldn't waste time. She'd been fooled. Cable wanted her trapped on the roof. Her only guess as to why was so that he would have plenty of time to go after Jack and Zaun. He wanted to fight them one on one. Since he'd been beaten by Zaun, maybe he felt wounded and needed to prove himself by taking them all out on his own, one at a time. Why he hadn't offed her, she didn't know.

Maria stared across the roof at the exit on the opposite side. She could try the door, but it would most likely be locked. And if it wasn't, it would be because Cable wanted her to head that way.

She spun around, headed to the edge of the roof and saw the rope dangling a few feet away from the backside of the roof access's roof. Cable wouldn't expect her to take that route, so that's the route she decided upon. But she couldn't reach it without leaning way out, and even then she'd probably have to leap. Jumping out to grab the rope was one thing, but leaping sideways along the building was another. Not enough spring or a slip, and she'd plummet to the ground. She would need to get onto the roof of the stairwell which was about eight feet up.

Standing back at the door, she studied the structure it was attached to. She returned the Glock to its holster, took a few steps back, and then ran. She jumped up as she approached the door and was able to get her right foot onto the handle. A moment later, she lost her footing, slipped, and fell.

Dusting herself off, she realized the run-and-gun approach wouldn't work, and stretched her leg, wedging her foot in the door handle. With her leg muscles straining, she grunted and jumped up. Her fingers brushed the lip of the roof, but she managed to get two of them to catch.

Barely holding on, she adjusted and got a better grip by using all her fingers before latching on with both hands and pulling herself up so that she was able to sling her right foot onto the roof. From there, she wormed her entire leg over the edge and used her thigh to haul herself up and onto the flat roof.

Laying on her back, she took a second to catch her breath, and then was up and ready to move. The rope appeared to be securely tied off to some kind of hook that had been hammered in place. She tugged on it and found it was indeed safe to use, then walked over to the edge.

The wind howled against her. She shivered as a chill made its way down her back. She pulled the coat tighter, wishing she'd worn gloves. They would make the climb down easier and quicker. She would have to move hand over hand, quickly but cautiously. If she fell and broke a leg, they'd all be screwed.

Gunshots sounded again. From her position, Maria had a view of the entire highway and surrounding area. She saw Jack, arm outstretched. It jerked and a zombie nearing him fell. Maria smiled, knowing Jack was alive and holding is own. But undead dotted the landscape and more were coming. There were no large packs, just stragglers coming from the woods around the mall. But that didn't mean the place wouldn't be overrun with the undead soon. Right now, there were enough of them to cause a problem. She couldn't see Zaun and was grateful he was staying put. And he hadn't fired the Browning, at least to her knowledge. He was the ghost; the unseen backup. Maria nodded, seeing things were still okay.

Kneeling at the roof's edge, she grabbed the rope and moved into position to descend.

CHAPTER 2

Cable stood on the landing above the stairwell, the darkness welcoming. He'd seen Maria coming long before she arrived at the building. He could have picked her off at any time, but then he'd seen her scuttle across the field and make her way to him. The game was on. The trio was separated. She'd come alone, leaving Zaun under the overpass and Jack to fend for himself. Originally, he had thought she might go back and attempt to rescue Jack which would have allowed him to injure her with a precise shot to the arm or leg. Nothing life-threatening. He'd then have Zaun all to himself and another chance to defeat him in battle. Maria would be claimed as his own, and they'd start a family somewhere. Life was all about second chances. The world was different now; no rules, no laws, and no order. But things rarely went as planned. So the hunt was on.

Jack was alive, but severely injured, and he'd been bitten. It wouldn't be long before he was a member of the undead. Cable wanted to kill him with his bare hands, but as long as he got to Zaun, he'd be satisfied.

After tying off the rope to the roof, he shimmied down and followed Maria inside, keeping back so she wouldn't hear or sense him. He never thought things would go so easily. He had imagined with her training that she'd prove to be a greater adversary that she was, but it was still fun. She went right for the roof as he'd expected. He was glad she hadn't checked all the offices, or she would've found the undead he stashed. In small numbers they were easy to handle and easier to kill. After grabbing two of the rotting bastards, he got them to the roof and almost burst with laughter when the gunshots sounded. He only wished he could have seen her reaction.

With both roof access doors locked, he knew she'd eventually find the rope. Maria was a survivor and wouldn't give up. He heard her against the door, and then on the roof of the stairwell, his plan working wonderfully.

Giving Maria a minute, figuring that was enough time for her to be in the act of descending, he left the stairwell and climbed up to the roof. He went over to the edge and looked down, now holding his hunting knife in his hand. Maria was only a quarter of the way down. Depending how she hit the ground, she could suffer a broken ankle or leg or arm. Or she could land okay and just suffer some bruising. But if he let her get much lower, she'd surely receive little pain at all.

Not wanting to waste another second, he got on his hands and knees. "So nice to see you again, Maria," he said. The woman looked up, her eyes wide with panic. He saw her go for her gun, but he was faster, already prepared, and sliced the rope with his knife.

Maria let loose a substantial yelp as she plummeted to the ground. She landed on her side with a thud, the snow fanning out around her.

Cable pulled his sidearm, ready to put a bullet into her calf, but hesitated. She wasn't moving, clearly knocked unconscious. He turned and hurried down the stairs to the second floor. If he didn't have to injure her, it would be better for him. With little in the way of medical supplies, there was the chance her wound would get infected.

He deserved a second chance in this new world. He was a killer, no doubt, but he could change. Use his skills to protect his wife and children. Maria would come around; she'd have to. Once she saw what a great father he was, she'd learn to love him—or at least learn to need him.

He raced down the second floor hallway and took the stairs that led outside and to the front of the building. As he made his way past the storefronts, a hint of doubt crept into his mind that she'd still be there. Maybe she had been playing possum and was gone, or was waiting for him to come around the building and blow him away.

With gun in hand, he peered around the corner of the building and saw her lying in the snow. He relaxed and approached her, feeling confident, until he heard the shot and was thrown into the wall.

CHAPTER 3

Zaun kept an eye on Jack and Maria, using the rifle's scope to get a closer view of the goings on. Jack didn't move from his position, making the task of watching him much less difficult than following Maria, who often went out of his sights. Not being able to rescue Jack or help Maria more directly was eating away at him. At least Jack was conscious and defending himself, taking out any undead that came his way. But Zaun didn't think he looked so good. His friend's shooting arm dropped quickly to the ground after every shot, as if holding up the weapon was a tiring chore. Jack sat against the snowmobile and hadn't moved since he'd crawled over to it. Zaun needed to get to him soon.

Maria was on the roof. He'd seen Cable slide down a rope. He'd wanted to take a shot, but was afraid he'd miss and screw up whatever Maria had going on over there. He needed to trust her. He moved his eye back to Jack, making sure the man was conscious, and when he moved back to check on what Maria was up to, he saw her on the ground. The rope was gone. He hadn't seen what happened, but guessed it had been cut when Maria was using it. Cable had known she was there.

Scanning the building, he didn't see Cable. Anxiety built. Maria wasn't moving, and he wondered if she'd been shot. He didn't remember hearing any gunshots, so he didn't think so. It was time for him to get over there and help her.

About to get up, he spotted Cable as the man shot out of a door in the front of the building. Before he knew it, Cable was standing over Maria, gun out.

It was now or never. He held his breath and took aim, lining up the scope's crosshairs with the psychopath's head. Damn, he was shaking. It was cold and he was nervous. There was a chance he'd miss such a small target. If he hit, it would be a kill shot, but if he missed, Cable would most likely escape. Maybe even kill Maria.

Zaun adjusted his aim, focusing on Cable's torso, a much larger target. He let out his breath, relaxing and pulled the trigger. The gun jerked and roared. Cable spun like a top and crashed into the wall before he slumped to the ground. Zaun kept an eye on him for a moment, seeing no movement. He stood and hollered in triumph, then hobbled over to the snowmobile, stashed the rifle securely and started the machine.

After pulling on his helmet, he hit the throttle and raced out to Jack where a number of undead were approaching.

"What took you so . . . long?" Jack asked, laughing. His thick pant leg—where the bullet had ripped through—was darkened, rich with blood. The snow around him was a rich shade of crimson. With his visor up, Zaun was able to see how pale Jack's color was, the flesh whiter than the outlying landscape.

"Had a few things I needed to take care of," Zaun said as he dismounted the sled. Sliding his sword from the sheath, he sliced the first zombie he encountered, removing its head easily. The next bot-controlled corpse—a hardly decomposed female with long blonde hair and missing half her face—Zaun put down with a thrust to the head. He quickly removed the heads from three more undead before returning to Jack.

"Let's get you out of here," Zaun said, and bent to help Jack up. Jack cried out.

"Okay, buddy," Zaun said. "Let's try something else." Zaun got behind Jack and dragged him across the snow, leaving a trail of red behind, and over to the snowmobile. He lifted Jack onto the seat and positioned him.

"Damn, I feel like shit," Jack joked. He slumped back, Zaun grabbing him before he fell off the seat. He held onto Zaun. "I'm okay."

Zaun wasn't so sure and wondered what was going to happen when they raced out of there. "Hold on a sec," he told Jack, then gathered his backpack, gear and weapons, and strapped them to the back of his and Maria's supplies. For a moment, he thought the sled was going to tip backward, the mound of supplies overwhelmingly high, but it was nothing compared to the snowmobile's front-end weight.

Zaun jumped on the sled, reached back, and pulled Jack's arms around his waist. He interlocked his gloved fingers and told him to hold on with all he had. Keeping a hand tightly over Jack's crossed fingers so they wouldn't come apart, Zaun hit the gas and headed to the strip mall.

Jack cried out in pain with every dip and bounce. Zaun felt his arms go limp a few times and strained to hold onto him. Finally, Jack slipped free and tumbled off the sled. Zaun hopped off and scooped him up, ignoring his friend's angst. This time, Zaun sat Jack against the mountain of supplies, strapping him in place with a few bungee cords. "Sorry man, but you're little more than cargo now."

Zaun got back on the sled and sped over to Maria. She was still lying on the ground, not moving. Cable was gone, but there were splatterings of blood in the snow and against the brick work of the building. Damn it, he hadn't killed him. But at least he'd wounded him.

Zaun glanced around, making sure the psycho wasn't near, and saw a trail of blood and bootprints leading to the rear of the building. The desire to run Cable down and finish the job tore at his soul. He could easily finish the guy off, but at what cost? Jack's and Maria's lives? He couldn't risk it.

Keeping the snowmobile engine running, he crouched next to Maria and flipped up his visor. He was afraid to move her. "Maria," he said. "Maria." He bent to her ear and told her she needed to get up. Removing his glove, he felt for a pulse and breathed easier when he found one.

Zaun gently patted her cheek. When she didn't respond, he shook her, needing her to wake up. Her eyelids fluttered before opening. "Zaun?"

"Yeah, it's me," he said, smiling.

"What . . . ?"

"You took a spill off the building."

She moved to sit up and yelped in pain. "My shoulder . . . It's dislocated."

"Shit. What do I do?"

"Where's Cable?" she asked, glancing around.

"I shot him. He took off."

"Okay. Help me sit up." Maria held out her uninjured arm and Zaun assisted her. She groaned, jaw muscles flexing. "Rotate my arm, slowly."

Zaun gripped her wrist and moved it in an arch until it was straight up in the air. Maria was groaning, but told him to keep going. He pushed out and down, Maria grimacing more.

"Pull and push now, fast," she said.

Zaun yanked outward, then shoved the bone back in place. Maria screamed for a second, then held her arm.

"It's back in place," she said. "Damn that hurt." She looked up and finally saw Jack, her face brightening. "You got him."

"Yeah. But he's not doing so good." Jack was slouched on the sled, head tilted, clearly unconscious. '

Maria and Zaun climbed onto the exceedingly crowded snowmobile. "Where to?" Zaun asked.

"Head to the Galleria mall. We need shelter and have to assess Jack's condition."

Zaun took off, Maria keeping an eye behind them for Cable, but by the time they crested the highway via the overpass, the view of the strip mall was gone.

The mall entrance doors were locked, boarded over. Undead roamed the parking lot and were coming their way. Zaun drove around, checking various entrances, but all were sealed up, making him wonder if someone else had taken up residence in the place. But the structure was huge. The place was the size of a small city. It had four floors and multiple parking structures, a movie theater, IMAX theater, Best Buy and a shitload of other stores. Attached to the mall up on a small hill was a Home Depot. Zaun decided to head there.

The front doors were smashed out, gaping holes for anyone or anything to come and go through. The snow around the entrance was undisturbed. A good sign. Zaun drove the snowmobile inside and killed the engine a few feet from the entrance.

"We need to get this entrance boarded up," Maria said.

Zaun agreed, and unless the wood supply had been raided, they could easily seal up the entryway. But if a horde formed outside, they would need something more secure than sheets of plywood and 2x4s.

"All those undead down in the parking lot and everywhere else are going to head here. Damn snowmobile is loud."

"We'll just have to get some heavy stuff to blockade the entrance with," Maria said, wincing and holding her shoulder as she looked around.

"I have an idea," Zaun said. "Help me get Jack and our gear off the snowmobile."

"Why?"

"We need a distraction, a target for the undead to swarm on. I'll ride out and blow it up, then sneak back here."

Maria eyed him and appeared to be thinking. She turned and headed to the blasted-out entranceway and surveyed the parking lot below. Zaun followed.

Most of the undead were heading toward them, still a ways off. With the deep snow and their slow shambling, the zombies wouldn't reach the Home Depot for a while, but by then more would have gathered, the small group becoming a small horde.

"I'm not wasting the snowmobile and risking us being stranded here," Maria said. "If we need to get out of here in a hurry, we'll need it."

"Then we better get to stopping up this huge-ass gap."

CHAPTER 4

The store's interior was pitch black, the flashlights' beams unable to breach the vastness of the place. Aisles disappeared into the abyss, both in height and length. But having visited numerous Home Depots, Zaun and Maria found the lumber section with relative ease, the air filled with the scent of machine cut wood.

They loaded sheets of plywood, 2x4s and long 2x6s onto orange-colored flatbed carts, and then ushered them over to the entrance. Maria's shoulder throbbed with pain, causing her to cry out a few times, but she dug deep and worked through the angst, knowing their lives depended on her and Zaun.

Finding saws, hammers and nails, they quickly constructed a frame and support structure, then nailed plywood in place. The makeshift wall stood 8 feet tall—the length of the plywood—and completely blocked the entrance. But it was hardly strong enough to keep out a mass of undead should they come barreling into the place.

Next, they piled bags of cement onto a number of flatbed carts and wheeled them over as extra reinforcement. It was still nowhere near what Maria wanted as far as a blockade, but it would have to do.

Of course there was another entrance, but the glass doors were intact. They managed to get them closed, and Zaun painted them over in black spray paint to keep anyone or any*thing* from seeing inside.

Unable to see out of the blockaded entrance, Maria had no idea if the undead had arrived. Her shoulder pulsated, sending bolts of agony into her chest and along her arm. Damn it, she needed to rest.

"It's something," Maria said when they were finished. "But I don't know how long it will hold up against a large mob."

"I'll find more items to support it," Zaun said. "The glass doors too."

Maria thought about trying to cart over refrigerators—if the store carried them—or something of equal weight and size. But the task would only sap their strength, and they needed to be on their toes and ready to react. The store was only a temporary home anyway. As soon as Jack was able, they would be on their way.

"I think we're good for now," Maria said, sitting on a lawn chair and rotating her shoulder. "We need to take care of Jack and ourselves. We can go to the offices at the back of the store. Nothing should hear us back there. If the undead were still after us, I think they'd have arrived by now."

Zaun nodded, and they checked on Jack. His face was the color of paste and he looked gaunt—bags showing under his eyes, cheek bones more defined.

"Damn, he doesn't look good," Zaun said.

Maria tried waking him, but to no avail. Jack's pants were saturated in blood. She checked his leg wound, afraid of what she might find—the damage too great—and was surprised to see it wasn't nearly as bad as she'd thought. She shook her head, amazed. The bullet had gone through, the exit wound the size of a dime. Entrance wounds to gunshot victims were often small, but the exit wounds were larger, often gaping holes. It didn't make sense.

"There's too much blood for such a small hole," she said. "And if the bullet had hit the femoral artery, he'd be dead by now."

Jack had a lot of blood around his collar and down the front of his coat too. Maria didn't think much of it, until she unzipped his jacket and saw the source of the bleeding.

"Was he shot in the neck too?" Zaun asked, leaning in for a better look.

Maria studied the wound. Again, there was too much blood for what appeared to be a—

A chill ran through her.

"I think that's a bite mark," she said, swallowing, and then it all became clear. The pale skin, the gaunt appearance. Jack was infected, turning. She stood fast. "We need to Taser him."

"Wait, are you sure he was bitten?" Zaun asked.

"That's a bite mark on his neck, Zaun. No doubt. It explains why he looks so dead."

"Even if that were true, it takes time. He was only bitten . . . what? A short while ago."

"Even with massive blood loss, he wouldn't look like this. Remember what Reynolds said? The bots adapt and evolve. We've already seen examples, how they're harder to kill with electricity. Maybe now they are finally doing what they were designed to do."

"You mean they're healing him?"

"It would explain the wounds being so small. But I also think the little bastards are draining him. Sucking him dry in order to heal the damaged parts. It's the only thing I can think of that explains his gunshot wound along with why he looks like he's turning."

Maria pulled her Taser from her backpack and aimed it at Jack's chest.

"Wait," Zaun said. "What if he hasn't healed enough? Still needs the bots?"

"It looks like they've done a lot of that already. I'm afraid if we wait, they'll kill him. His body will have to do the rest on his own." She pulled the trigger and sent two darts into Jack's chest. His body trembled as electricity coursed through him. She held the trigger, hoping to fry every last little devil.

She couldn't believe the things were actually healing him, doing what Reynolds had initially set out to have them do. Now she could only hope she could kill them, otherwise all the healing would be for nothing and Jack would slowly be eaten from the inside out.

When the Taser charge died, she checked his pulse. "Shit," she said, and hurried to load another charge into the Taser.

"What?" Zaun asked.

"I think the shock was too much for his heart," she said, her voice cracking. She fired the Taser again. Jack's body trembled. She didn't hold the trigger long this time, only wanting to give him a quick jolt in hopes of starting his heart.

She pressed her fingers to Jack's throat. Dropping the Taser, she began chest compressions, and then checked if he was breathing. When she realized he wasn't, she gave mouth-to-mouth before returning to chest compressions.

"Come on," she yelled.

"Shoot him again," Zaun said, and handed her his Taser.

Maria felt tears streaming down her cheeks. With everything they had gone through, to lose Jack now just wasn't right—wasn't fair. They'd fought through so much. He deserved to find his sister, to know if she'd survived.

She shot him again, and then wiped her wet cheeks. Afraid to check his pulse, she did so with a trembling hand. Finding one, she exhaled. "He's alive." She closed her eyes for a moment.

"We need to get him warmed up," Zaun said. "The place is probably large enough so that a small fire won't smoke us out, at least not for a while. What do you think?"

Maria was about to agree when an idea hit her.

"Wait here," she said, and took off with a flashlight. She scoured the aisles, looking for portable heaters. The floor was littered with products, the shelves apparently raided for certain items. She kept searching, not sure where such a thing would be located, until she saw a bunch of mini propane tanks. Next to them were the portable, non-electric heaters that operated on propane. Finding a shopping cart a little ways down the aisle, she loaded in five heaters and a number of propane tanks, and then hurried back to Zaun and Jack.

They wheeled Jack and their belongings to the back of the store where offices and the employee break room were located. The flashlight beams cut through the intense darkness as they searched for undead. Jack was then lifted off the flatbed cart and laid on a couch in one of the offices. Propane tanks were inserted into the portable heaters and then the heaters were placed around the room. The heating coils cast a soothing orange glow over the place, making the flashlights unnecessary. The cold air was quickly warmed, Maria and Zaun having decided a smaller room would be easier to heat.

Maria dressed Jack's wounds using supplies from the first aid kit they had taken from Cliff House. When the room reached a comfortable level, she shut off two heaters, wanting to reserve the other propane tanks for later use.

"So, what do you think?" Zaun finally asked, sitting in the high-backed office chair behind the cherry wood desk.

"He's alive," Maria said, flatly. "We just have to keep an eye on him. I'll check his wounds tomorrow. Keep them clean. Hopefully the bots healed him enough so that he'll be okay."

***

After a while, Zaun told Maria he was going to check on the entrance and look for supplies they could use. He went to the break room. The snack machine was void of anything edible, the glass smashed out. The soda machine had been pried open and robbed of its product.

He headed to the front of the store next and checked the blockade. Pressing his ear to the wood, he listened, but was unable to hear anything save for the howl of wind. He was careful not to make a sound for fear a group of undead was just outside. For now, he guessed the front of Home Depot appeared to be one solid wall. The undead must have lost interest in them as they trekked across the parking lot tundra, the snowmobile going too far ahead for them to keep up. He knew they'd follow an object for miles if said object remained close, like when they had led the undead up the mountain. But he had no idea what they'd do if they lost sight of it.

He thought about finding a ladder and climbing up so he could see over the wall, but didn't want to risk making noise, having learned his lesson about being too curious back in the city.

He checked out the line of cash registers, searching for any candy that might've fallen under the racks—the shelves empty—but found nothing. There were only last minute impulse items as the stores called them, things shoppers saw and purchased on their way out—screwdrivers with multiple head attachments, tape, batteries, gift cards and whatnot. He wasn't worried about food. They had plenty for now. But finding something chocolatey would have been nice.

Something banged behind him, causing him to spin around, Glock in hand. It was only the wind slamming into the wooden wall, but it made him think of Cable. The psycho was still out there. He'd had the man in his sights, chest centered. But somehow he'd missed the man's vital areas, as impossible as it seemed. Shooting someone, especially from a distance, wasn't like a video game. Still, he'd hit the bastard and sent him into the side of the building where he slumped to the ground and lay unmoving. So how could he have crawled away?

Easy, stupid, a voice in his head answered. *You only wounded him.*

Zaun sighed. He was frustrated, but told himself that Cable had mostly likely crawled away to die. There'd been a lot of blood at the scene.

He didn't want to spend his time thinking about the psycho-killer, but not doing so would be foolish. He had no idea if Cable was alive and in what condition. If the man was well enough to travel, and if so, would he know where they went?

Zaun thought not, then realized how easy it would be to follow the snowmobile tracks to the Home Depot. Unless it snowed, it would stay that way too. And the sky had been clear with no indication of bad weather moving in.

Zaun grabbed a flatbed cart and searched the aisles for more items to place behind the wall. The more, the better. The entrance might not keep out a thinking person, a person like Cable who could climb over it or smash through it with a vehicle, but he could at least further ensure against anyone crashing through with ease.

He came to the paint section and found a plethora of five-gallon cans and loaded them onto the cart until it was full. Loaded down and heavy, he managed to sluggishly push it to the blockade wall and shove it up against the bags of cement. He then loaded another two carts and did the same. There was a lot of weight now against the wall, ensuring its hold should something happen.

Next, he headed to the gardening department, surprised to find so many items in stock, considering the epidemic had started just before the winter. He wheeled seven barbecue grills in front of the black spray-painted glass door. He then returned to where the cement bags were stacked and loaded a few carts up, placing them behind the grills. It wasn't nearly as secure as the wooden blockade, but anything that might hinder intruders had to be better than nothing.

Tired and hungry, Zaun headed back to Maria. He ate some deer meat and told Maria to take a nap. She eyed him and he knew what she was thinking.

"You can trust me," he said. "I won't go anywhere, and if Jack wakes or it looks like he's in trouble, I'll get you up."

Maria got up and walked behind the desk. She pulled the chair out and sat, then put her feet up on the table. "I can't promise I'll sleep, but I'll at least rest a little." She sat back and closed her eyes.

A few minutes later, she was sleeping.

CHAPTER 5

Cable had made his way back inside the building. His enemies had left, taken off toward the Galleria mall. He kept his injured arm steady, not knowing what kind of damage he'd sustained. Needing warmth, he built a fire on the roof just outside the roof access door, allowing the small stairwell landing to be heated while the smoke escaped into the air. The fire's fuel source was a combination of natural tree branches he'd collected since arriving at the building and pieces of wooden furniture.

After removing his jacket and upper body undergarments, he inspected his shoulder. The bullet had torn through the deltoid muscle, leaving a fleshy, bleeding mess. His entire jacket sleeve was soaked through. Pain radiated up his neck and down his arm, but the limb was usable. He raised the appendage and rotated it, checking the joint to make sure it wasn't affected. White hot pain engulfed the area, but that's all it was— pain. There was no hindering damage, nothing to affect his ability to operate as usual as long as he fought through the pain and kept the wound from becoming infected. He'd been lucky and would have one hell of a scar.

He assumed Zaun had taken the shot, clearly no sniper. If Maria had taken it, he would be dead or almost so. She was military trained.

Thinking about Zaun, Cable couldn't believe the man had resorted to using a firearm against him, and a long-range one at that. They were hand-to-hand combatants, meant to duel the oldest way known to man. Their previous encounter had been legendary. Yes, Cable had lost, but it was only a battle, not the war. The true winner would be the one left alive. Zaun had failed. Had made a crucial error in letting him live. A second and final go was necessary, but now . . .

Initially, Cable had foreseen them in another fight, their skills tested for one last time, but then Zaun had gone and changed the rules by using a firearm. Now if Cable had had the opportunity, he'd have to consider taking it—killing Zaun by way of the gun, close or from afar. The end was the end, regardless of how it happened. Of course, he'd prefer to best the fighter one on one, and if the opportunity presented itself, he'd take it.

Cable set the blade of his hunting knife in the fire. Once the steel turned orange, he pulled the weapon out using cloth around the handle and pressed the steel against the exit wound. The flesh sizzled as the wound was cauterized. He cried out as pain overwhelmed him, the smell of his burning skin keeping him lucid and from passing out. He repeated the process on the entrance wound, a much smaller hole, but the pain was no less. Sweating, he gathered snow into a plastic baggie he'd found in one of the offices, and iced the seared flesh, the cool white stuff providing a temporary numbness from the hurt.

He sat, ate a can of beans and added more wood to the fire. He thought about searching for painkillers, but didn't want to waste his energy. Pain was pain; nothing more, nothing less. In this new world, it was something he was going to have to learn to accept, just like everyone else. Pills and shots were a thing of the past.

He'd taken a lot of damage over the last month, the aches seeming constant. Planning on living a long and healthy life in this new world was another thing one couldn't count on. But after he'd won, took out Zaun—for Jack was surely dead by now—and made Maria his, unless he decided to kill her, he would settle down somewhere for a while, rest up and fully recover.

Eventually the undead would die off, their bodies rotting away to nothing more than bone. There would always be one or two about, people always died, but the majority would be gone. The world would be left vacant, vast and ripe for the taking. The disease moved quickly and would wipe itself out eventually, like diseases of the past had—smallpox, the Black Death and whatnot.

Thinking about the two undead he'd trapped in that office, he was bothered. They appeared fresher than most he'd run into, as if newly turned. However, their clothes were torn and filthy, indicating they'd been undead for a while. For a moment, he wondered if they had gotten better, somehow healed, but quickly shook off the notion. Things were only going to get better for him.

A cleansing of the earth and a way to restart mankind was happening. A sort of rebooting of the planet.

Cable laughed at himself, knowing he'd watched one too many science fiction movies while in prison. He lay back, letting the warmth of the fire wash over him. He needed to think of his next move.

With Maria and Zaun injured, he figured they would likely hole up somewhere nearby. If anything, they'd want to stay with Jack while he passed, maybe even bury him, though the frozen ground would make such a task nearly impossible. It would be at least a couple days before they moved on, to where he didn't know, but move on they would. So he had to do something before he lost them. In the morning, he'd head out and follow their tracks, and if they were in the Galleria mall, he'd find them and kill them, or get killed trying.

CHAPTER 6

Cable awoke to sunshine the next morning. His shoulder throbbed and moving his arm hurt like hell. He checked his wound and found no sign that it was infected. In fact, it was already scabbing over. He put a fresh bandage over it, then gathered everything he wanted to take with him into his backpack and left it on the second floor in one of the offices. When he finished with Zaun and Maria, he'd come back for it. Maybe head south to warmer weather.

From the roof, he surveyed the surrounding area, able to see for miles in most directions. He used his rifle's scope for close-up views. All in all, there was no sign of his prey. A few undead roamed the open tundra here and there. But nearer to the Galleria was a small horde of about thirty zombies. They must have chased his prey when they left, then lost them and went into their semi-sleep mode, or whatever it was that the undead did when there was nothing to eat. Having seen the boarded up mall entrances and the huddled group of undead near the bottom of the hill that led up to the Home Depot, Cable guessed that's where they had gone. Of course, they could've gone past the home improvement store and into the woods beyond in hopes of finding a neighborhood where they could hole up in a house. But he didn't think so. Not with everyone injured. They'd want immediate shelter.

Next, he studied the ground below, found the snowmobile tracks and followed them as far as his eyes could see, then used his rifle's scope to follow them farther and saw that they led to the Galleria's parking lot. From there, as he'd expected, the tracks headed up the hill to the Home Depot.

Heading downstairs—armed with his .45, a Heckler and Koch machine gun strapped to his back, and a hunting knife—he exited the building in a rush to get to his snowmobile and came face to face with a pack of undead.

More annoyed than surprised, he growled expletives and withdrew his handgun. The rotting things must've been right up against the building and under the lip of the roof, making it impossible for him to see them from his perch.

Raising the .45, a Kimber Tactical, he shot the closest zombie in the forehead and splattered its brains across the others behind it. Without hesitation, not a shred of fear for their undead lives, they stepped toward him, arms out, reaching. Cable paused for a moment, thinking two of the zombies were alive, their faces unmarked and colorful. Then he saw the vacant looks in their eyes and the worn and filthy condition of their clothing.

Adjusting his aim, he quickly downed the remaining four. With no other undead in the immediate area, he didn't care about making noise, and in fact, enjoyed getting to shoot something.

He stood over the corpses, wondering what the hell was going on. The others were pale, gaunt and rotting, with gashes along their arms and face, one with a missing ear.

Doesn't matter, he thought. Good shape or not, they were all mindless flesh eaters that needed to be put down or used to his advantage.

Moving on, he headed to the tree line where he had stashed the snowmobile. After dusting the snow off the cover, he rolled it up and stuffed it under the seat. The machine started with a push of the button, and Cable was cruising across the overpass within moments.

Undead from all around took notice and worked their way toward him. Cable raced along, following his prey's snowmobile's tracks. He reached the home improvement store in no time. With the deep snow impeding the already slow undead, it would be a while before they reached him—if the stiff-legged things could even climb the hill.

He took notice of the walled entrance, wondering if it was something recently built or had been up for a while. He drove the snowmobile within a few feet of it, keeping a watchful eye on the blockade. The building had no windows, so he wasn't worried about someone seeing him, and the wooden wall had no apparent slots or cut outs where a gun could be shot from.

Leaving the engine running, Cable hopped off the sled and walked up to the barrier. The air was ripe with the odor of freshly-used lumber, and then he understood the blockade had recently been erected. He pushed on the plywood in a couple of places and found the wall solid. He nodded to himself, knowing what he had to do.

Glancing over his shoulder, he saw that the pack of undead was approaching the incline. A few stragglers were working their way over from the highway too.

Removing his jacket, Cable tore the right sleeve off his long john undershirt before zipping the garment back up. He unscrewed the gas cap on the snowmobile and shoved the sleeve inside. After allowing it to soak in the flammable liquid for a minute, he pulled the sleeve out and approached the wall. The smell of gasoline wafted around him like an unseen demon waiting to wreak havoc.

With the dripping piece of fabric, Cable whipped it at the blockade and sent splashes of gasoline across the wood. When he was satisfied with the task, he laid the sleeve out along the bottom of the wall, lit a match from the book of matches he carried, and watched the wood ignite. He stepped back as flames burst to life. The wall quickly became an inferno as well as the target he needed the undead to head toward.

Climbing back on the snowmobile, he turned the throttle, sped off and parked behind a large box truck. From there, he had a good view of the burning entrance and would remain unseen from people exiting or undead arriving.

CHAPTER 7

Maria checked on Jack as soon as she woke. She'd managed to nod off for a little yesterday while Zaun kept watch. The day had crept along and the excitement level was equivalent to snails racing, but she'd take it that way. Her worry for Jack was high and kept her from truly being able to rest.

Jack's skin was pale again, his face gaunt. She removed the bandage from his neck wound and saw that it was nothing more than a scratch, letting her know the bots were still active in his system. She didn't need to check his thigh.

"Damn it," she said.

"What?" Zaun asked, sitting up, yawning.

"Jack's wounds are almost completely healed," Maria said. "Which is good, but it also means the bots are still active."

Zaun was fully awake now and got to his feet. "What do we do?"

"Shock him again."

"Wow, he looks terrible," Zaun said, running a hand over his hair.

"Yeah, the little devils are eating him alive while they heal him. Stupid fucking things."

Maria grabbed her Taser.

"Are you sure his body can handle it?"

Maria shrugged. "We have no choice. He's probably in the best shape he's ever been in, considering the bots healed every piece of him. But at the same time, they're taking away from his healthy parts. I really have no idea what's going on inside him. Just get your Taser ready."

"We've got to wake him. He probably needs to eat. Give the bots what they need." He moved toward Jack.

Maria held him back. "First, we kill the things. He'll wake when he's ready. To do so now might kill him, if he'll even respond."

Maria pointed the Taser at Jack and fired. His body tensed. She held the trigger until the charge died. She imagined the bots squealing in agony as they fried, but at the same time wondered if she was even hurting them. Jack had been Tasered twice already and the things were still functioning.

She checked Jack and found that he was still breathing. Zaun handed her his Taser. She fired again, holding the trigger until the charge was depleted. When she checked him, he wasn't breathing. She then felt for a pulse, found none, and began CPR. A few seconds later, he was back.

"Damn it," she said, kicking a cardboard box in frustration. "This shit's getting old."

"What if . . ." Zaun began. "What if we can't kill them?"

"Then we keep trying."

"Should we shock him a third time?" Zaun asked. "You know, because two didn't work before."

Maria shook her head and exhaled noisily. "I want to, but I'm afraid we'll kill him. Maybe in a few—" She stopped, her head cocked. "Do you smell that?"

Zaun sniffed the air like a dog smelling its owner's dinner cooking on the stove. "Smoke. That can't be good."

They looked at each other, worry spreading across their faces.

"Something's definitely on fire," Maria said.

They grabbed their M4s, sidearms already on their person, and headed out of the office. As they worked their way to the front of the store, the smell of smoke grew stronger, and then they saw the flickering of orange-yellow light along the walls.

Exiting from the aisle at the far right side of the front of the store, they saw the flames from afar and rushed to the cashier area. The barrier they'd built was an inferno, flames licking the white-painted cinderblock wall above where a banner caught fire.

"What the hell?" Zaun said. "How did this happen?"

One of the paint cans exploded, sending arches of liquid flame over the area. Smaller fires ignited in the checkout aisles. A withered and dead fern went up in flames.

"Cable," Maria said. "It's got to be him."

Zaun shook his head. "No way. He's dead."

"We didn't see a body."

"I'm telling you, I shot him. He crawled off to die. No way he survived, and even if he did, he couldn't be in any condition to do this."

Another paint can exploded. Then another. Zaun and Maria backed up, a wave of heat falling over them.

She, too, had assumed Cable was dead. There had been no time to make sure, to hunt him down. She knew Zaun had hit him, but it obviously wasn't a mortal hit, unless this fire fiasco wasn't caused by the madman, but by someone else.

"This whole place is going to go up in flames if we don't put it out," Zaun said.

The fire was already too big. There was no way that spraying a couple of fire extinguishers was going to douse it. They would need a team of them.

"I've got a crazy idea," Maria said. "C'mon."

"Where are we going?" Zaun asked as he chased after her.

She grabbed a shopping cart and raced past a few aisles before turning down one. "I think I remember seeing them here . . ."

"What?" Zaun asked, sounding frustrated.

"Fire extinguishers. I could've sworn they were in this aisle."

Reaching the aisle's halfway point where an intersecting lane cut through the middle of the store, they went left and tried another aisle. Maria took the right while Zaun the left.

"Here," Zaun said a moment later.

Maria hurried over to him with the cart, her and Zaun's flashlight beams reflecting dully off the rows of red-colored metal canisters. They quickly loaded the cart and headed to the front of the store where the inferno blazed.

"What now, we start spraying?" Zaun asked.

Maria shook her head. "Normally, yeah, but we're going for a miracle. There's no way we'd be able to put this out by using these things in the traditional manner."

More paint cans exploded, sending arcs of flames everywhere, including Zaun's arm. His jacket sleeve caught fire. He cried out and waved his arm around like a fool. Maria shoved him to the floor and sprayed his arm with one of the fire extinguishers.

"Weren't you ever taught to stop, drop, and roll?" she asked.

Zaun got to his feet. His jacket arm was melted and charred, resembling some strange flesh-eating disease.

"Shit, that was scary," he said. "We need to do something or get the hell out of here."

"Grab a fire extinguisher," Maria said, holding the one she had used on Zaun.

Zaun picked one up. "So what now?"

"We're going to toss them in and let them explode. The contents of each canister should coat the area and smother the flames."

"Will that work?"

"No idea, but we have to try something."

On the count of three, they began tossing the fire extinguishers into the blaze until the cart was empty.

"Now what?" Zaun asked, stepping back.

"We take cover."

CHAPTER 8

Cable heard a series of popping sounds from within as the small horde of undead approached the Home Depot's entrance. The fire was raging now, licking the surrounding cinderblock walls as if starved. The undead moved toward the fire as expected. It didn't matter what the movement or sound was, the seemingly mindless creatures were easily led. Cable looked on as if watching a live action movie unfold, interested in how things were going to turn out. The wall was weaker now, if not gone. The undead would walk into it. The first ones would catch fire but continue on and break through the blockade. Flaming zombies heading inside would cause such havoc, igniting items and other things, making his prey's dwelling a hazardous place. They'd have no choice but to fight, waste their ammo and energy dealing with everything. Then he could sneak in and hunt.

But something strange happened as he looked on. A few of the undead did as he thought they would and walked right into the fire. They stood in the blaze, showing no sign they cared that they were melting away. But the others had stopped walking about ten feet from the inferno. Half the group moved closer, but none would walk into the wall. They all stared on, and a few took steps backward.

Cable's mouth hung open. If he didn't know any better, he'd swear they were showing signs of caution or fear. Something was going on with them. A change. It explained why they looked better. But how was that possible? It was as if they were becoming human again.

Cable heard crashing sounds from within. The undead heard it, too, their heads tilting like a curious dog. The scene spooked him and sent a chill throughout his body. Cable's euphoric mood at being able to hunt his prey turned to dismay. He couldn't have the undead become human again. He needed them to stay mindless, rotting and flesh-eating. The new world was perfect the way it was. He ground his teeth, feeling frustrated and worried. The emotion was odd, frightening.

The wall exploded.

The undead were knocked back as flaming debris tore into them, ripping arms and legs from torsos, like undead human bowling pins hit with a bomb. Heads and other pieces littered the ground, the snowy earth now cleared to the pavement. More explosions occurred, and Cable felt the ground shake. More debris shot outward along with a white substance that expanded like foaming soap bubbles out of an overfilled washing machine.

Only a third of the horde rose back to its feet. Charred and smoking, jaws blown off, fingers scattered along the ground, they muddled around, not seeming to know where to go or what to do.

More popping sounds came from within. The noise caught the zombies' attention. They moved as one toward the entrance, the fire completely out save for a few smoldering items, and then Cable saw something shiny and red, part of a canister that appeared to have been blown open. A piece from a fire extinguisher. He grinned. His prey was smart. Cunning. Using fire extinguishers as a way to not only put out the fires but as weapons too. Genius.

As the undead entered, gunshots sounded and the zombies fell. Cable knew then that his prey was alive and well; at least well enough to defend themselves. By the sound of the gunfire, there was more than one shooter.

When the shooting stopped, he waited to see if someone would show themselves, and when no one came from the building, he moved out from behind the truck.

Crouching low, he moved toward the other building's entrance, and then worked his way over to the blown out one. The smell of burnt wood, rot and chemical foam surrounded him, the mixture of odors nauseating.

Breathing through his mouth to avoid the horrendous smell, he moved into the entranceway's overhang, staying close to the wall. He took a few moments to listen for the sound of the others. Hearing only the crackling of a few small fires as they dwindled out of existence, he peeked around the corner and peered into the gloomy store.

Dead bodies littered the floor. A single bullet hole decorated each of their heads, the shots clearly aimed. Even under such extreme conditions, Maria and Zaun had maintained their poise. Impressive.

Dented paint cans lay about, lids blown off. The immediate area was a collage of colors, as if a rainbow had exploded. Charred and burnt wood was scattered about, everything covered in white foam.

He didn't see anyone or hear their voices.

Stepping farther inside, he was careful to avoid stepping on wreckage. One wrong move would alert his prey to his presence.

A faint glow of light shone from the right. He could see it through the aisles. Flashlights. Cable moved farther in, passing the cash registers and into the store's main walkway. The sunlight only reached so far before he was shrouded in darkness. He continued onward toward the lights.

Reaching the aisle, he heard the sound of hollow clanking, like empty propane tanks knocking together.

"How many do we need?" Zaun asked.

"Just load up. We'll use some for defense, the rest for keeping the heaters running."

So they had a heat source, Cable thought. Most likely propane. A great idea and one he'd make his own once he dealt with them.

He thought about shooting blindly down the aisle, hitting one of the tanks and setting off a huge explosion that would surely kill his foes. A man with nothing to do might choose this method of eliminating his enemy, but Cable was playing a game of war, and he didn't want to lose all that propane—the portable heaters would surely come in handy.

"That will do it," Maria said, and as she turned around, her flashlight blasting the aisle ahead with light, Cable ducked back into the next aisle where the darkness swallowed him up.

The squeaky sound of wheels rolling filled the air and he waited, Kimber Tactical at the ready. From his crouched position, he watched the two stroll by, each of them pushing the cart.

As soon as the cart was out of view, he came from his hidey hole and crept up behind them. Sunlight engulfed their forms as they made it to the checkout entrance. They were such easy targets. Two pulls of the trigger and they'd be dead. His finger itched at the possibility of eliminating them. Maria was on the left. Zaun the right.

"Move and you die," Cable said, pointing the .45 at Zaun. If he was going to spare anyone, it was going to be Maria. He'd break her. Train her. Give her children and make her love them. She'd want to keep them safe. Would need him around and learn to love him. It would take time, but in this new world, time was all they had.

The cart stopped moving.

"Hands in the air," Cable said.

They did as they were told.

He inched up behind Maria and conked her on the back of the skull. She let out a moan before collapsing to the floor. Zaun flinched, but Cable had the barrel of the .45 pressed against his temple.

"You piece of shit," Zaun said.

"Just relax," Cable said. "Wouldn't want to have to shoot you." He slid Zaun's handgun from its holster and tossed it down the aisle. He then slipped the M4 that was strapped to Zaun's back from his body and threw it into the darkness. Cable patted Zaun down. Finding no other weapons on the man, he took a few steps back.

"Turn around," Cable said.

"If you're going to kill me, just do it," Zaun said.

"Oh, I do plan on killing you, just not yet. Unless, of course, you leave me no choice. Now, turn the fuck around."

CHAPTER 9

Zaun turned around and faced Cable. He thought he'd see a beaten and bruised man, bloody and ragged. But instead, he saw a man who appeared fine, healthy.

"You look disappointed," Cable said.

"I shot you."

Cable nodded. "Yes, you did. Just a flesh wound, really." Cable rotated his shoulder. "Hurts like a bitch, but I'll manage."

"I should've killed you when I had the chance."

"But you didn't. The fates see it fit to have us do battle again which is what we're going to do here today. Set the record straight. See who wins the war."

"You want to fight?" Zaun asked.

"We're not on the playground. A couple of kids duking it out. We're trained killers. This is life and death. A war between two warriors."

Zaun couldn't believe it. This maniac wanted to fight it out instead of simply putting a bullet into him. The guy had clearly lost his mind.

Cable removed the machine gun strapped to his back and slid it down the aisle, keeping his handgun trained on Zaun. "Before I disarm myself, we'll need to make sure Maria here doesn't interfere. Find something to tie her up with. I'll give you a minute."

Zaun glanced around. He didn't see anything he could use. "I don't know where to look."

"That's okay," Cable said. He aimed the gun at Maria. "I'll just kill her, and then we can begin."

"Wait," Zaun said, holding out his arms and stepping in front of her. "I'll find something, but I'll need to check the aisles."

"Get going then. Time's running out."

Zaun picked up the flashlight and was ready to run down the aisle where the guns had been tossed, when Cable said, "Not that aisle."

Zaun nodded and took off down a different lane.

"Try anything funny and Maria gets a bullet to the head," Cable threatened.

Zaun searched the shelves for something he could use to tie up Maria. He passed by screws and piping before reaching the wide aisle that cut through the store and separated the smaller aisles into two parts. He turned down another aisle, seeing it was stocked with boilers and other equipment, and moved a couple aisles down to where he found pliers and bolt cutters. He continued along and came across screwdrivers, but they were all sealed in hard plastic packages. He could've easily hid one down his pants and used it as a stabbing weapon when he fought Cable, but there was no way he could get the package open quickly and quietly. Next was the hammer section. Most were too large to hide on his person, but then he saw a small, ball-peen hammer. He pulled it from the hooks it was hanging on and shoved it into the small of his back and covered it with his shirt and jacket.

"Time's almost up, Zaun," Cable yelled.

Picking up his pace, Zaun reached the end of the aisle and turned down the next one. The flashlight's beam fell on coiled ropes of thick orange and green-colored extension cords. Too thick, he thought and moved the light farther along until he came across smaller, thinner bundles—the kind of extension cords a person would use every day in their home. Thin enough to be used to tie someone's hands together. He grabbed two handfuls and returned to Cable.

"Now tie her wrists behind her back, then secure her ankles. Make sure you do a good job, because if I have to worry about her interfering with us, I'll just make the problem go away."

Believing Cable's words, Zaun made sure Maria wouldn't be able to escape her bonds. When Zaun was finished, Cable had him back away and checked the job he'd done.

Maria came to as a few moans escaped her lips. She appeared groggy, but it only lasted until her eyes fell on Cable.

"Get the hell away from me," she shouted.

Cable stood back and laughed.

She looked at Zaun. "What the hell is going on?"

"Just sit tight. Once I kill this psycho, we'll be all right."

"I like the confidence, Zaun," Cable said. "Glad to see you're up to this. How's the leg by the way?"

"Let's just do this."

Cable shook his head. "Take off the jacket."

Zaun did, tossing it away.

"Turn around."

Zaun rolled his eyes, but did as he was told. He felt the cold steel of Cable's gun press against the back of his skull as he was patted down. "What's this?" Cable asked, his hand on the hammer. The nail-whacking tool was removed from Zaun's possession.

"I'm very disappointed in you, Zaun," Cable said, taking a few steps back. "First, you use a gun; upped the stakes between us. Now, we agree to hand to hand combat, and you had this hammer on you."

Zaun didn't know what the man was going to do, so he quickly said, "I didn't know if I could trust you. I remember you pulling a blade on me during our last meeting. Wanted to be able to even the odds if I needed to."

"Ahh, so this was a 'just in case' item?"

"Yeah," Zaun said, knowing his words meant nothing to Cable.

"Face me," Cable said.

Zaun turned around, expecting to be whacked in the face with the hammer, but found himself catching it after Cable tossed it to him. He looked at it, confused and worried.

"For attempting to cheat, I want you to smash one of your hands. Just once, but make sure it's hard, or I'll be forced to have you smash Maria's hand too."

"Afraid to fight him?" Maria asked. "You almost had him in the basement of that house, Cable. Don't you want a fair fight?"

Cable chuckled. "I did, but Zaun here seems not to want one. So he's going to be penalized." Cable raised the gun and pointed it at Maria, but spoke to Zaun. "Smash one of your hands with the hammer or I'll shoot her. You've got until I count to five."

Zaun got on his knees and placed his hand on the frigid floor.

"One . . ." Cable said.

Zaun raised the hammer, his brain screaming at him to stop.

"Two . . ."

He stared at his left hand, hoping he'd be able to do it hard enough. Satisfy the madman. But if he did it, he'd be at a severe disadvantage."

"Three . . ."

Zaun glanced up and saw Cable staring at Maria, smiling. The maniac's focus was on her. Cable loved seeing her turmoil.

"Four . . ."

Zaun swung his arm forward and let the hammer fly. Cable's face went slack as the object approached, as if he couldn't believe what he was seeing. Zaun lunged forward, wanting to come in right behind the hammer, Cable only a few feet from him.

Unable to move completely out of the way, the hammer smacked Cable above his left eye, the thud deafening.

The gun went off.

Zaun didn't know where the bullet had gone. He didn't feel anything and was on Cable in seconds, forcing him to the ground.

Straddling the lunatic, Zaun used both his hands to control his enemy's gun arm. He took a punch from the man's free hand, but the blow had little power behind it. They wrestled for the weapon, Cable refusing to let go. Zaun tried twisting and then slamming the man's hand against the ground, but his effort proved ineffective. Cable punched him again, then latched onto his throat and squeezed. Zaun lost the ability to breathe and managed to tear himself away from the man's grip while keeping the gun hand pinned down. Not knowing what else to do, he leaned down and sank his teeth into Cable's wrist. The man howled as his hand open, and Zaun was able to knock the gun away.

Cable punched Zaun in the throat. Zaun felt his strength momentarily leave, allowing Cable to heave him off. He landed next to the big guy, and knowing he needed to get away from him, rolled.

Cable got to his feet and headed toward Zaun.

"Watch out," Maria yelled.

Zaun looked just in time to see Cable's foot coming at his face. He covered up and absorbed the blow, pain exploding in his forearm. Zaun wheezed in a breath, his throat semi-closed from the hit he'd taken there. Another blast from Cable's boot hit him in the stomach, knocking the wind from his lungs. Needing to get out of that position, he rolled as if on fire, and then jumped to his feet.

Cable was on him in seconds, swinging a punch his way. Zaun ducked and moved sideways, then came up with a kick to Cable's liver. Cable answered with a kick of his own to Zaun's thigh.

Breath coming easier, Zaun launched an open palm into Cable's chin and forced the man's head back, then sprang forward with a knee that landed in the man's groin. Cable hunched over and Zaun jumped up with his other knee and nailed Cable in the nose, feeling it crunch under the impact. The psycho flew backward and tripped over Maria's legs.

Zaun looked around for the gun, saw it laying against a piece of charred 2x4. He hurried over to it and scooped it up, then spun around, expecting Cable to be charging at him, but instead saw the man holding a knife to Maria's throat.

CHAPTER 10

Jack awoke with a searing hunger in his stomach. Opening his eyes, he quickly sat up, confusion befalling him. The last thing he remembered was lying against the snowmobile, dying and trying to keep himself from being eaten alive. Now he was in an office, a soft orange glow illuminating the place. He wasn't cold. In fact, he was comfortable, warm. He saw the source of the soft glow and knew heaters had been placed around the room. Instead of feeling safe, he panicked. None of this made sense. Where were Maria and Zaun?

Then he remembered that he'd been shot.

Jack ran a hand over his thigh. There was no pain. He stood and pulled his pants down, needing to see the flesh. A bandage covered his skin. It wasn't soaked with blood. He didn't see a drop. He tore off the dressing. His leg was normal-looking, as if nothing had happened to it. He brought a hand to his neck, felt another bandage and ripped it off. The skin below was smooth.

Jack pulled up his pants. He suddenly felt weak, legs wobbly. He collapsed back to the couch, a wave of dizziness falling over him. He took a moment, pain engulfing his stomach.

He needed to eat.

He saw his backpack, along with Zaun's and Maria's over by the door, and could practically smell the food within the bags. Like a ravenous creature, he crawled over to his pack and pulled out two MREs and a bottle of water. He prepared the meals, knowing he needed both. He wanted to eat them as they cooked, hardly able to wait. Normally, he'd think to ration, but the thought didn't even enter his mind. As soon as they were ready, he gobbled down the food. When he was finished, he waited a few minutes. Still needing to eat, he made another MRE.

He allowed the food to settle, hardly believing he was able to eat so much and not feel like he was going to explode. But he felt good, energized.

For a moment, he wondered if he was dreaming.

Getting to his feet, he saw a Home Depot banner across the wall. He didn't remember anything past his being shot. Somehow, he'd been brought to where he was, but how in the hell was he uninjured yet alive? He figured with his wounds healed and his incredible hunger, that he'd been asleep for some time. A month maybe. It seemed impossible, but how else could he explain it?

He needed to find Maria and Zaun.

He went over to the door and opened it. The hallway was pitch black. He grabbed a flashlight from his pack, strapped on his gun belt holding the .45, then grabbed his shotgun and headed into the hallway. There was another office across from him, and next to that was a larger room. There was a sink, cabinets, a counter, chairs and vending machines. An employee breakroom.

He moved to the end of the short hallway where the cavernous warehouse store opened up. His flashlight proved but a faint glow in the vast darkness. The ceiling and aisles seemed to extend into an endless void. The smell of lumber surrounded him. Sheets of wood took up the aisle he was standing in.

He started forward, ready to call out to Maria and Zaun, but decided it might be best to keep his mouth shut. He had no idea what was going on.

The air was much colder outside the office. He wished he'd taken his jacket, but he wasn't about to return for it now. If he had to go outside, he'd consider going back.

He heard voices as he neared the end of the aisle and killed his flashlight. Peering around the corner, he saw figures standing in a huge sunlit area. The entrance to the store was open. From where he stood, he couldn't see who they were.

Still shrouded in gloom, he moved forward, knowing he couldn't be seen, and when he finally came close enough, he saw someone on the ground, a large man and a smaller one. Moving closer still, he was able to see Zaun and . . . Cable? Then he saw the gun in Cable's hand.

He couldn't believe it. How the hell did that maniac follow them? Then he knew. It had been Cable who shot him. Had to be. The figure on the floor was Maria. He wondered if she was dead, then heard her speak and relief flooded through him.

Wondering what his best course of action was, he watched as the men talked. Cable took something from Zaun, then handed it back to him. There was no way Jack could charge in. And with only a handgun and a shotgun, there was no way he could aim a shot and not take a chance of hitting Zaun—especially in his current position. Zaun was closer to him, partially blocking his view of Cable at times. He needed to—

Zaun got down on his knees.

Jack froze, straining to see what was happening. Then he saw the hammer in Zaun's hand, raised above his head. First Cable takes the thing from Zaun, then gives it back, but to what end?

It didn't matter. He needed to get over there and take out Cable.

He hurried back down the aisle—flashlight on, but covered by his hand so only a sliver of light shone—until he came to the wide aisle that cut across the entire midway point of the store.

A gunshot sounded.

Jack's mind raced with horrendous images of Cable blowing Zaun's brains out. He'd been too late. He should have charged straight in and caused a distraction. Went in firing. Something, anything.

He raced along, no longer covering the light. He needed to see, to vault over items in his way. The closer he came to the end of the corridor, the more sunlight allowed him to make out things ahead of him. He slung the shotgun over his shoulder and pulled his sidearm.

"It's over asshole," Zaun said.

"You have no honor," Cable said. "Drop the gun or Maria gets a new smile."

Jack slowed as he approached the end of the aisle. He saw Cable, the man's back to him. The madman was holding onto Maria. About ten feet away Zaun stood, pointing a gun.

Jack had his sights on Cable's head, the .45 aimed at it. He moved to his left a little, clearing Maria's head of Cable's, the silhouetted outline of the two creating a two-headed monster. Jack could shoot, end it all, but there was a chance the bullet could hit Maria too.

"You've got until I count to 5, then this bitch dies," Cable said.

"Then you die too," Zaun said.

"Doesn't matter. The pain of her death will haunt you forever. I'll eternally be in your thoughts. You'll never shake me."

Jack crept up, avoiding the rubble on the ground as best he could. Then something crunched under his right foot, the sound echoing like a gunshot. He froze, wincing.

Cable spun around, keeping Maria in front of him. He had a knife to her throat. His eyes went wide, a mask of utter disbelief on his face.

"Impossible," he said.

Jack knew a window of opportunity had opened. He saw Cable's body relax, the big man obviously stunned. Maria's eyes met his. Unspoken communication took hold between the two. She yanked down on Cable's knife arm, clearing the blade from her throat. Jack took a moment to make sure his aim was good, then fired.

Cable's head jerked back. Maria tore herself free as her tormentor's body collapsed to the floor. Zaun ran up, stood over Cable and put another bullet into his head. He looked at Maria, saw she was okay, then looked at Jack. "You're up."

Jack nodded. "Yeah, I sure am."

Maria hugged him. Then Zaun joined in.

When they were finished, they backed up and looked at each other.

"How do you feel?" Maria asked.

"Numb and a little confused," Jack said. The adrenaline rush was wearing off and weariness was settling in. He wobbled, and Zaun caught him.

"Whoa," Zaun said.

"I'm okay," Jack assured him.

"You look better," Maria said, smiling.

"Good to hear," Jack said, scratching the back of his head. "Now could someone please tell me what the hell is going on?"

CHAPTER 11

After being stripped of his weapons and jacket—Jack wearing it to keep from freezing—Cable's corpse was dragged outside and laid among the strewn landscape of dead undead. It was Zaun and Maria's first up-close look at the undead that had been blown from the wall. Some were crispy, but most were still as they had been before the explosion, but in more pieces. Fresh blood stained the snow as if some of the undead had been alive—which was impossible as everyone knew. The more likely scenario was they had been recently turned. Maybe a group of survivors had been hiding in the mall, were overrun and turned before they finally made their way outside. When the zombies spotted the fire, they came over only to meet an early undead death.

Maria mentioned how the two undead she had come across on the strip mall's roof appeared fresh, too, though their clothes said otherwise. Studying the bodies in front of her, the same thing could be said. Not all the undead were in 'good' condition. A few were emaciated, stripped of flesh in areas where bone could be seen. The flesh on those undead was cracked and gray, old-looking.

"Based on the clothing," Maria said, "I don't think many of these undead are newly turned. I think something's up with the bots."

"Yeah," Zaun said, nodding. "Something's definitely up with them." He looked at Jack who was feeling hunger pangs again.

"You think they're keeping them fresh?" he asked. "Maybe even healing them?'

Zaun chuckled. "You've got no idea, Jack."

Maria cleared her throat.

"What aren't you telling me?" Jack asked.

"It's better we talk inside where it's warm, and we'll be hidden," Maria said. "There may not be any up and moving undead out here now, but it doesn't mean more won't show."

They headed inside and went back to the office. The heated air was almost overwhelming. Jackets were removed and a sense of security fell over the group. Jack could tell they all felt truly safe for the first time in a while. He ate while Zaun and Maria talked about what happened after Jack had been shot, from Maria hunting down Cable, to Zaun rescuing her, to the blockade they built, to the fire, and then finally to Jack's condition.

"So, we're still not sure you're bot free," Maria said.

Scraping the MRE bag clean, Jack said, "It makes sense then."

"What does?" Zaun asked.

"Why I'm so damn hungry." He went on and told them how he already ate two MREs and had woken ravenous.

"It definitely might explain it," Maria said. "The bots are working. Healing you. In turn, they need food, or more correctly, your body needs nutrients that the bots are taking."

"So I'm still infected," Jack said, crumpling up the bag. "But I feel great. I mean, my wounds, they're gone."

"Let's just hope that once you're fully healed, not just the outside, but whatever internal injuries you might've suffered, that the bots will stop doing whatever they're doing. Hibernate or something."

"Yeah, or I'm going to eat us out of everything in no time."

For the rest of the day, the group talked, rested and ate. Jack's appetite returned to normal by evening. They kept watch in four-hour shifts, each one as uneventful as the next.

Come morning, the group packed up. Jack felt normal. He wasn't overly hungry at any time, wasn't tired or hurting, just his regular old self.

"Should we try something?" Zaun said. "You know, to see if the bots are still in you? See how they operate?"

"What do you mean?" Jack asked.

"Give yourself a small cut on the arm. See if it heals; see how you feel."

Jack was nervous enough having gone through all that he'd gone through. He didn't want to test anything. If the bots were hibernating, inactive, whatever, he didn't want to take a chance and activate them. He feared they were only going to change, further evolve over time. Maybe next time, they'd cause more damage than his body could handle. But he knew he couldn't go on with the rest of his life not knowing about himself, especially with how things were. Injury was a part of life now, it seemed.

"So you're thinking better to test out how I am going to react now while we have shelter and food?"

"Yeah," Zaun said.

Jack looked at Maria, wanting her input.

She stared at him, then nodded her head and sighed. "As much as I don't want to treat you like a guinea pig," she said, "a small incision might not be a bad idea."

So it was decided. Jack rolled up his sleeve, and after cauterizing his knife, sliced a two inch cut along his forearm. Blood drew. The group waited, watched. Little by little, the blood dried up, a scab formed. It took about thirty minutes. Jack felt no hunger pangs, nothing unusual. He picked off the scab, which flaked away like nothing more than dried milk, and his flesh was unmarked below.

"Damn, that's incredible," Zaun said.

"No, that's science and a madman's vision coming true," Jack said. He was more than glad the wound healed without complications. In a way, he wondered what would happen now. If he was mortally wounded, would he simply heal as long as he had food to keep his body alive? Would the bots stay active inside him forever? If he was repeatedly shocked, would the bots eventually die? Be altered? These were all unanswerable questions, at least for now. Only time would tell, which bothered the hell out of him. He thought about the 'fresh-looking' zombies outside and the blood. If the bots healed the living, would they heal the undead?

"Guys, this is scary shit," Zaun said, then slapped Jack on the shoulder. "But I'll take it over you being dead, man."

Jack couldn't argue with that. He nodded and said, "True enough, but I'm still a little worried about what this means. Not only for me, but for the undead. Will they be harder to kill? Stay around longer? Or in attempting to heal them will the bots inadvertently wither away their bodies to nothing?"

Maria sat behind the desk, feet up. She was bouncing a small rubber ball against the wall. "We'll just have to wait and see, but for now, we treat everything as usual. Keep you, Jack, from injury. Make sure we have food and kill any undead that come our way."

After that, the group finished packing and loaded up the snowmobile. Jack knew it was going to be a slow, cramped ride, having only one snowmobile to use. And there was still a ways to travel in harsh conditions, despite the current weather showing clear and sunny skies.

Loaded down and ready to move out, Jack spotted another sled near a box truck as they were leaving. The only thing he could guess was that the machine had been Cable's. With another snowmobile to use—the key in the ignition—the gear was evenly distributed between the two machines. They went back inside and gathered extra propane tanks, heaters, some tools and a gasoline can that they filled by siphoning the gas out of an old Mustang parked in the lot.

They headed up the Thruway. On occasion, they had to go around vehicles in their way or speed past roaming zombies. One time they had to circumvent a small herd by traveling through a field. They saw no people about. The only signs of life came from a few houses in the far distance, smoke billowing from the chimneys.

When they came to the Harriman exit, they got off the highway and headed down route 32, a single-lane road that cut through the wooded area of Central Valley and its small towns. Undead were about in the towns, but nothing they needed to worry about, and they kept on, the hum of the engines a constant, normal sounding part of the journey.

When they reached Angola Road, they went up a steep incline and made their way along the backroad, the heavily wooded area thick with untouched snow. Jack imagined how everything, living and unliving, heard them, with the entire mountainside's undead population turning their heads and making their way toward the whining engine. It made him want to go faster, but knew it was just his mind playing with him.

They stayed at a steady pace, the speedometer reading forty miles an hour. When they came to Furnhill Road, they turned onto it and traveled a mile up a steep incline before arriving at Jack's sister's house.

It was a two story abode with a two-car garage. The house sat on an acre of land and was surrounded by a thick tree line of ferns and oaks—the oaks bare—that separated the neighboring houses.

Jack hopped off the sled. He tried lifting one of the garage doors, and when it didn't open, he tried the other, but to no avail. They killed the engines, looked around for any approaching undead. The surrounding snow was undisturbed like a sheet of freshly laid icing.

"This place is like a ghost town," Zaun said, stating the obvious.

"Good," Maria said. "Let's hope it stays that way."

They went around the right side of the house, the property having a slight incline to it, and found the snow-covered set of stairs that led up to the front door. Finding it locked, Jack wrapped his knuckles on the door. "Sara? Are you in there? It's Jack." He knocked again. With no answer, he and the others went around to the back and tried the door there, but it was locked too. Then he saw that one of the den's windows, the room at semi-basement level, had been boarded over.

Movement sounded from the bushes behind them. Jack spun around, M4 ready, and saw a zombie shambling toward them. The knee-deep snow greatly slowed its movement. Zaun pulled his sword and said, "I got it."

Jack and Maria pried off the piece of plywood from the window.

Darkness filled the den within, and Jack hoped not to smell the putridness of rotting flesh. Instead, he smelled vanilla and felt warm air fall over him. Excited, he called out. "Sara, it's Jack. Are you in there?"

The sound of a shotgun being cocked echoed in his ears a moment before he was staring into the barrel of one. "I'd advise you to move on, stranger," a voice said from the darkness.

Jack didn't recognize the voice as Carl's, but asked if it was him anyway.

"No Carl here, young man. Just us armed men."

"I don't want any trouble," Jack said, seeing Maria creeping along the side of the house, making her way to a window. "I'm just looking for my sister, Sara Warren. She lives here."

"No one here by that name now. In case you haven't noticed, things have gone and changed quite drastically around here. Found this house after mine burned down. Claimed it as my own, considering it was empty and all."

The man sounded older and had said he was one of a group of armed men. But Jack didn't think so, especially after hearing him say he had claimed the house as his own, as in singular.

"Okay, my friend," Jack said and backed away, hands up. The M4 hanging off his shoulder slipped and he went to catch it.

The man's shotgun fired, a flash of light exploding from the darkness.

Jack was thrown backward, pain wracking his side.

Maria returned fire, shattering the glass window adjacent to the one that had been boarded over. A cry from inside the house rang out. Then, another blast from the shotgun sounded.

Jack glanced down at himself and saw a huge hole in his jacket. The snow was speckled with crimson, feathers floating toward the ground like soap bubbles.

"Shit," he said, going numb.

Zaun rushed over and dragged him to safety.

Maria tossed a flashbang grenade into the house and covered her ears.

A few seconds later, the bomb went off and a flash of light brightened the darkened room for an instant.

"How's Jack?" she asked.

"I . . . don't know," Zaun said.

The snow around Jack was further reddening.

"Good thing I come equipped with my own healing system," Jack said, coughing up blood.

"You weren't supposed to be the one who gets hurt," Zaun said. "Remember? Just in case?"

"Guess we'll find out what the bots do this time . . . If I'm savable." He tried to stay awake, to hold on, but suddenly his body teemed with unbelievable pain, as if his insides were being shredded, and he passed out.

CHAPTER 12

"How is he?" Maria asked, keeping an eye on the blown out window.

"Looks bad," Zaun said.

Knowing Jack would need immediate shelter and food, the house was a must have. If someone—maybe *someone's*—was holing up inside, that meant it was most likely stocked with supplies, including food. Whether or not it was worth risking their lives was another question, but based on what just happened, she didn't think a group of armed hostiles were inside.

Maria headed over to the back door, blew its handle out, then kicked it open. She waited for gunfire from whoever was inside, but none came. "Drag Jack over here," she called to Zaun, and he did, leaving behind a trail of bloody snow.

"We clear the house, then bring him inside," Maria said.

Zaun turned around and yanked his sword out. "Just a second," he said, referring to the zombie still working its way through the snow.

Maria raised her rifle and fired, blowing the bot-controlled brains from its head. There was no need to keep quiet now, guns had been fired. Zaun slid his sword back into the sheath and took up his M4.

They entered the house and were in a short foyer with a washer and dryer set along the left wall. A door was on the right. Maria opened it and saw the front end of a Chevy Blazer shrouded in gloom and knew she'd found the garage. She closed the door and moved into the house. A hallway went left, and she assumed she had thrown the flashbang into that room. To the right were stairs leading up to another level.

Maria paused. The house was still, as quiet as she could remember a place being. She motioned to Zaun that she was going left. Zaun nodded and followed, watching the stairs.

She looked into the room and saw an elderly man on the floor, apparently unconscious. He was wearing black khakis and a tan sweater. A bushy white beard covered his face, his skull bald except for the Caesar crown of long, white hair around his head. A shotgun rested a few feet away from him. The room was warm, and then she saw why—a small wood-burning stove rested in the center of it. Flames danced behind the ceramic window. A pile of logs lay next to smaller pieces of wood, the floor beneath dirty with chips of bark. A collection of water jugs took floor space in front of the television.

She moved in and quickly saw that no one else was present. Zaun stood by the doorway. "It's all clear," Maria whispered as she checked on the elderly man. He was alive. She pulled out a couple of zip ties, secured his wrists together, and then his ankles before dragging him to a corner across from a computer desk. Next to the desk was a door. She shouldered her rifle and pulled her Glock, wanting it for close-quarter action, and yanked the door open. Before her was a closet, the shelves stocked with canned goods.

She closed the door and returned to Zaun's side and in a whisper, she said, "Let's bring Jack in here, then search the rest of the house."

Jack was still bleeding, a pool of red sloshy snow where they'd left him outside. Zaun and Maria carried him inside and to the den where they laid him on the couch.

"This all looks too damn familiar," Zaun said, shaking his head.

Maria nudged him and held a finger to her lips. Zaun nodded. Jack was stripped of his jacket and shirt. The wound looked like something had taken a large bite out of his side. She didn't think there were any important organs located there, the wound not quite reaching the liver. She had no idea what body parts the bots needed in order to work at their best, but if they operated the undead, she assumed just the brain.

After bandaging Jack's side, they checked the rest of the house and found it unoccupied. Nothing was in ruin. One of the bedrooms had its drawers open, a couple of them on the floor as if the person had been in a hurry to leave, but that was all. If this was Jack's sister's house, which she had no reason not to think it was, the woman had headed elsewhere. They needed to wake the old man and find out.

Back downstairs in the living room, Zaun set up the portable heaters while Maria found a hammer and nails in the laundry room and boarded up the broken windows. She'd thought about moving to another part of the house, but aside from not wanting to move Jack again, the wood stove could come in handy. For now, though, it would not be used, the remaining fire inside left to burn out. She didn't need a signal letting others know someone was alive inside. She'd seen and dealt with too much to take a chance that someone might come along and be a problem. At night, they'd use the stove. And if they wound up staying long enough to where they used up all the propane during the day, then they would use the wood stove sparingly.

Maria stood over the captive. "He's just a frightened old man. All alone."

"Yeah, and he shot our friend," Zaun said.

"I know." Maria didn't know if it was the man's age, that he was alone, or just a culmination of all the violence she'd seen, but she actually felt bad for the guy. At the same time, she wanted to put a bullet into his brain—take no chance of another psycho entering their lives. Old didn't mean feeble or kind.

Tending to Jack, she didn't know what to do. Let him be or repeat how they treated him in the Home Depot. His cheeks already appeared sunken in, his flesh paler. The bots worked quickly. It had only been about an hour since he had been shot.

"I think we need to shock him," she said.

Zaun stood next to her. "Okay."

"I mean, if the bots did heal him the last time, really healed him, fixed him up to the best Jack he could be, then he should be able to handle the shock better than before."

"Makes sense."

Maria took out her Taser and exhaled noisily, not knowing if letting him be was the better course. Maybe he needed more time to mend, and by shocking him she'd hurt his chances at surviving. For all she knew, the bots were even stronger now, and shocking him would be the best thing. She just didn't know anything for sure. Her only hope was that the little devils were the same, maybe even better, smarter, and would know not to kill their host. Take only enough from Jack to heal him, at least enough so he could wake and consume food so they could continue to heal him.

That was wishful thinking, and she knew it.

Pointing the Taser at him, she fired and held the trigger until the charge died. She checked him for a pulse and found a steady one and breathed easier.

"We're good," she said.

"Going to hit him again?"

"No. Let's wait and see what happens. Keep a close eye on him."

Zaun nodded. "I'm going to keep a lookout from the upstairs windows. Just in case."

"Good idea."

Maria was proud of Zaun, remembering how at one time she hadn't much cared for him. She had thought he was a loser, a loose cannon that would get them all killed, and almost had. He wasn't like her or Jack. He was a free-spirit, spoiled, a don't-take-anything-too-seriously type of guy, and a drug addict. But he'd come a long way, helped her out a lot, became a man, a soldier, so to speak. She never thought she'd see the day he'd know the proper thing to do—and on his own—like keeping watch from the upstairs windows. Normally, that would have been something she had to tell him to do. It was a small thing, but it was nice to witness. If anything good did come from Jack's out-of-commission status, it was Zaun having to man up and take things more seriously.

Two hours passed by before the old man came to. Maria kneeled in front of him. He stared at her, a confused look on his face. Then recognition set in, fear along with it. His eyes went wide.

"Where's my wife?" he asked.

"Wife?"

"Please don't kill her. You didn't kill her, did you? Oh, no. Please. No."

"Quiet," Maria said, and threateningly raised her hand.

Zaun descended the stairs and came into the room. "Asshole's awake?"

"Your wife's not here," Maria said.

"You didn't find her?"

"No. Is she hiding in the house?"

"No. No. Not hiding." The man seemed relieved. "She's okay." He spoke softly, to himself. Then a look of concern crossed his face and he locked eyes with Maria. "Did you go into the garage?"

"No," Maria said, then wondered why they hadn't checked it out. Anyone in there would freeze after a time, but still . . .

She got up. "We need to check the garage."

"No," the old man shouted. He struggled to get up and wound up falling over.

Maria helped him to a sitting position. "Is your wife hiding in the garage, because if she is, she'll freeze to death."

"This guy's crazy," Zaun said. "Or has Alzheimer's."

The old man looked up at Zaun. "My name's Henry and I don't have Alzheimer's."

"You shot our friend, Henry," Zaun said, angrily. "You're lucky to be alive."

"Oh my," Henry said, his eyes falling to Jack. "I didn't mean to shoot anyone. I was so scared. Didn't know who you were. Saw the weapons and I panicked. I only wanted you gone. That man's sister wasn't here when my wife and I arrived. The place was empty and had all this food, so we stayed."

Maria stood and turned to Zaun. "Let's check the garage for people."

"No," Henry said, sounding desperate. "Please don't go in there."

"Is your wife in there or not?" Maria asked. "Because she won't last long, even if she's wearing a coat. I'm guessing she's older, like yourself?"

Henry nodded, tears falling down his cheeks.

"Just her?" Maria asked. "Is she armed?"

"It's only her. She's not armed. But she needs to eat. She's turning back. Becoming herself again. Please, don't hurt her."

Turning back, Maria thought, the man's words striking like a punch to the chest. Zaun must've caught on too because he looked at her with a raised eyebrow.

"What are you talking about?" Maria asked, facing the old man again.

He looked at her and exhaled, then explained how his wife had been bitten. The couple knew what that meant as they made it back to their home. He cleaned the wound, singed it with an iron and hoped all the measures would prove different than what they had witnessed. But then she, Mary-Beth, started showing signs. Getting sick. The military came through the area the next day. They were mowing down all the undead they came across and made announcements that survivors should make their way to Stewart Airforce Base, where a walled safe-haven had been erected.

"We couldn't go," Henry said. "They'd never let my wife in. They would shoot her as soon as they knew she'd been infected. I couldn't leave her. Whatever time she had left I was going to spend with her. So I stayed. When she finally passed and came back, I just couldn't do it. Couldn't kill her. I thought maybe there'd be a cure one day, something. So I kept her in our basement. I knew she was hungry, so I fed her."

"You what?" Maria asked astonished.

"Not people," Henry quickly added. "I fed her meat from our freezer. It was spoiled. She wouldn't touch the stuff at first, but then one day the meat was gone. I figured there had to be plenty of rotten meat in the surrounding houses. So I went out and gathered up as much as I could, and my wife ate everything I gave her. In these frigid temperatures, most of the meat I found was frozen, so there wasn't much of a stench. A few weeks ago, she started getting better. Her skin color returned, body filled out. Her eyes were clearer. I took care of her, washed her, changed her clothes. She even stopped attacking me."

"There's a fucking zombie in the garage?" Zaun asked, eyes wide.

"No," Henry said. "She's getting better. Turning back, becoming human again. Whatever this disease is, it's not permanent. Please, the woman you're looking for isn't here. Leave me and my wife alone. We're not hurting anyone. She's chained up."

"How did you come to find this place?" Maria asked.

"When I ran out of food, I went out searching other houses. I found food, of course, but nothing like what was in this place. Like most residences, this one was unoccupied by the living and had no undead in it, so instead of trying to gather the food little by little—I'm no spring chicken—and haul it home, I decided to come here. I wrangled my wife, forced her along and chained her up in the basement here."

"Watch him," Maria said. She grabbed a flashlight from her backpack and headed to the garage. The old man called after her, pleading with her not to hurt his wife. She opened the door and shined the light around the front end of the Chevy Blazer. The sound of chain links clinking against each other filled her ears. She moved around the bumper and into the open part of the two-car garage. Her flashlight beam came to rest on the old man's former wife.

Maria's mouth dropped open.

The thing didn't look like a zombie but more like a chained up woman, like some maniac's captive. A thick leather collar was around her neck, a six-foot chain leading from it to the cinderblock wall behind it. Her hair was full, wavy. Her cheeks weren't sunken or pasty, but full and lively-looking. There wasn't a noticeable mark on her. The man said he had taken care of her, which must've included changing her clothes, because they were mostly free of stains.

The zombie came forward as far as the chain would allow, arms reaching out. Its face contorted into an angry snarl. This was new, a sign of emotion. The undead had never made facial expressions before. Their faces were always vacant, unmoving and dead looking. They didn't fear, think or feel. But this one before Maria was proving otherwise.

She focused on its eyes, trying to see if there was life there, but saw only the eyes of a monster. If there was emotion in them, she didn't see it, yet.

She wondered what this meant. If the zombies were healing, getting stronger, did that mean they'd be human again or would it mean a harder enemy to deal with, one that could run and climb, maybe even think?

Maria returned to the living room and stared at the old man.

"Is she still alive?" he asked.

Maria didn't answer. In fact, she didn't know how to answer such a question. Maybe the thing in the garage was alive now, partly bot-controlled, partly operating on its own.

She walked up to him, pulled her knife from its sheath and cut him free of his bonds. "Get up and come with me."

"What's going on?" Zaun asked.

"How's Jack?"

"He's fine. Sleeping. No change."

"Let's go then."

They all entered the garage and stood in front of the man's former living wife.

"Damn," Zaun said, "she looks real. Um, I mean alive."

"She almost is, I think," Henry said.

The thing raised its arms again, but there was no snarling face this time. Its head tilted to the right, causing it to look as if it were curious. The corners of its mouth pulled upward, forming what had to be the slightest of smiles.

Maria couldn't believe what she was seeing. If she had doubt earlier, it was gone now. The thing was clearly showing emotion. Then it put one of its hands to its mouth and moaned.

"She's hungry," Henry said.

Maria's eyes widened and she found it hard to breathe. This was all too much. A communicating zombie. She thought about how it had snarled at her—because it hadn't recognized her. Now it was . . . happy? It felt secure because it knew Henry, like an owner coming home to his dog.

"Dude, this is crazy," Zaun said.

"May I feed her, please?" Henry asked.

Maria nodded. "Zaun, go with him."

The two left the garage. The zombie stared at her. Henry had said she was hungry. Maria stepped forward, just out of the thing's reach. Its face was slack. Maria held out her hand. The zombie stared at the offering, then raised its arms and latched onto her and tried pulling the hand to its snapping jaws. In no danger—the chain keeping the zombie's mouth a foot away from her—Maria yanked her hand back. She had her answer. The thing would eat human flesh.

She raised her gun and pointed it at the thing's head. Its mouth continued to bite. The gun had no meaning to it. It wasn't afraid.

Zaun and Henry returned.

The zombie stopped its aggressive actions.

"Hey," Henry shouted as he ran up to her. "What are you doing?"

"This thing tried to bite me. It isn't turning back. It's only getting stronger."

"No. I'm telling you. She's going to be the wife I knew again." Henry placed a plate of semi-frozen, rotten meat in front of the zombie. It didn't attack him when he drew close to it.

"Watch," Henry said.

The zombie reached down, picked up a good portion of the meat and shoved the putrid-looking stuff into its mouth. Maria expected it to immediately go for seconds like the undead always did, eating in gluttonous fashion. But to her surprise, the creature chewed until the food was swallowed. The zombie then went for more, repeating its human-like mastication.

When the plate was clean, Henry wiped his undead wife's face and cleaned the bits of flesh residing around her lips and on her chin. The zombie didn't attempt a hostile act. It just stood there, allowing him to do what he was doing.

"Amazing," Zaun said.

Maria replaced her Glock to its holster.

Henry picked up the plate and backed away. "See, she's okay."

Maria stepped up to the thing and held out her hand to it. The zombie looked at her, not the hand. After a minute, she stepped back.

"It's still dangerous," Maria said. "If you don't feed it, it will eat you."

The zombie let loose a grunt and a burp.

Maria couldn't believe it. Digestion?

Then she noticed its shoulders rise and fall. It was ever so slight, but it happened. Its abdomen was moving too. Why she hadn't noticed it before she didn't know.

"Is it breathing?" she asked.

Henry smiled. "Yes."

CHAPTER 13

After the incredible encounter, Maria and the others returned to the living room. Henry wasn't tied up, deemed to be a non-threat. He fed his former wife whenever he needed to. Maria watched over Jack and used the downtime to think. But there were no answers. The bot virus had indeed changed, drastically this time. The undead were healing to the point of becoming human again, but what that meant in the long run she had no clue.

In order to prolong the portable heaters' lives, the wood stove was fired up when the sun went down. Maria was still worried, but figured the chance of someone seeing the smoke under the cover of darkness was highly unlikely.

Maria and Zaun took turns keeping watch throughout the night. They both kept an eye on Jack, and by morning his wounds had almost completely healed. Maria had to Taser him only once having seen his body deteriorating the way it had in the Home Depot. But unlike that time, Jack's body hadn't needed to be resuscitated.

"Your friend," Henry said, "is he infected too?"

"Different story than with your . . . wife," Maria said. She started to tell Henry the story from the point of Jack getting shot as they snowmobiled up the Thruway, then decided with nothing but time, and wanting to share their tale with someone, she started from the beginning.

"Amazing," Henry said when she was done. "So you all were there from the beginning."

Maria nodded.

Jack stirred.

Maria went over to him. "Jack?"

He opened his eyes. "Damn, that sucked," he said, his voice barely above a whisper. "Thirsty."

Maria turned to get him water and found Henry standing before her, proffering a cup. She thanked him and accepted the offering before handing it to Jack.

Jack guzzled the water, a trickle dribbling down his chin. Maria helped him sit up a little. "How are you feeling?"

"Hungry."

Henry grabbed some canned corn and handed it to Jack, who asked, "Aren't you the guy who shot me?"

Henry's face faltered as he backed up a step. "I . . . um . . ."

"He's okay, Jack. It's a long story. Just eat."

And Jack did, finishing the canned corn, a can of black beans and an MRE. He lay back afterwards and relaxed as Maria told him about Henry.

Jack laughed. "Guess this confirms it. I'm a superhero."

Maria saw Jack's expression turn sour. He didn't say anything.

"What's wrong?"

"We came all this way for nothing. Sara's not here."

"If you're looking for the person who used to live here, you may be in luck," Henry said.

Jack looked up at Henry, his eyes intense. "What are you talking about?"

"When my wife and I arrived here, we . . . well, I, found a note. It was for a 'Jack'. I'm guessing that's you?"

"Yes," Jack said, sitting up, grimacing. He put a hand to his injured side, then lay back down.

"You're much better," Maria said, "but obviously still need to heal."

Jack nodded. "Please, mister, go on."

"Name's Henry."

"Okay, Henry. Please continue."

"There were a couple of notes pinned around the place. They were addressed to 'Jack.' It was signed 'Sara'. Said she went to the Air Force Base and to come find her there. Like I said, the military came through the area. She, like most, must have left."

Jack tried sitting up again, but Maria forced him down. "You need to rest."

"We're so close," Jack said. "I need to get over there."

"Give yourself another day. No point going out there injured. If she's at the base, she'll be safe. Another day won't kill you. In fact, it might just save your ass." Maria smiled.

"Jack sighed. "Fine, but we leave first thing tomorrow."

CHAPTER 14

Zaun was grateful Jack was on the mend. Tomorrow they'd be heading to the Air Force Base. Of course, it had been a month or so since the military had come around telling people to head to the base. Anything could have happened to the place since then. Maybe the base was up and operational, everyone inside doing well. Maybe they'd flown the survivors somewhere else, somewhere safe. Or maybe the place had gotten overrun by undead and was nothing more than most places—a zombie infested nightmare.

Zaun said nothing of his worries to Jack. He and Maria had discussed all the possibilities in private. Worst case, they'd simply have to move on. Zaun knew Jack hoped, even believed, that his sister was alive. But the reality was, she wasn't. It would be a shock. A devastation. But they'd be there for him. The same went for Maria and her family. She was intent on getting to them. Zaun couldn't blame her, and he'd go with her regardless of how remotely hopeful the outcome was. Like with his thoughts about

Jack's sister, Zaun said nothing about his concerns for Maria's family to her.

When it came time to feed Henry's wife—Zaun having no problem calling the zombie a her—he offered to get the meat. It was outside in a chest in the snow at the end of the property. The meat was covered in plastic wrap and sealed in plastic containers, Henry thinking it best to keep the odor from leaking out and attracting not only wild life, but the undead as well. Zaun would have used the meat to attract animals, because animals meant food.

He went outside and headed over to the chest, stopping short at seeing two undead pawing at it. There was a third zombie, but it wasn't doing anything except standing a few feet behind them, its arms at its sides.

Zaun drew his sword and approached. The crunch of snow caught their attention. The two decomposing zombies advanced toward him, their flesh far from healing. The third zombie didn't move. Zaun met the two with swiftness, a slice to one that removed its head and a jab to the other through its eye, the sword's tip popping out the back of its skull. He wiped the blade in the snow, then approached the remaining undead.

He came within a few feet of it, expecting it to attack, but it only shook and looked down as if afraid. He raised the sword, ready to strike. The thing glanced at him, its eyes went wide. For a minute, he thought it wasn't a zombie, but a person. A frightened woman. Then it hissed and ran off.

Zaun watched her go, amazed. He'd never seen a zombie run, let alone show that it was afraid. It had known Zaun meant to kill it. He chuckled, thinking it a good thing. If the undead were afraid of humans, like most animals were, then the world was about to become a safer place.

He opened the chest and grabbed a container of meat before returning to the house. He gave the food to Henry, who brought it to the garage, and then shared what had happened outside with Maria and Jack.

"Looks like we need to be ready for anything," Jack said. "If the undead are indeed becoming like wild animals, they could prove more dangerous, especially once they get used to seeing people. We don't know if they'll see us as food or as a threat."

Zaun could hardly believe how fast Jack had healed and at how much food he'd consumed since waking.

Things for the trio were finally looking better for a change.

CHAPTER 15

The bot-infested woman ran through the various yards and sections of forest on her way back to the log cabin house at the top of the mountain. She didn't worry about being quiet or seen. Most of the homes had been raided, the occupants taken and eaten by her people—the new people that had been reborn from the undead.

She did worry about the man with the sword. Feared him. He'd swiftly killed the stupid ones she had been with near the meat chest. He wasn't a coward like most other food. The food usually ran when they saw her, her people and the undead. If he had confronted her, she might have been able to defeat him. Rip him apart as she fed. But he'd had friends, and they could be as dangerous as him.

When she reached the log cabin, the nest, she was greeted outside by two guards. They grunted, and the one named Drek threw her to the ground. To return home without some form of bounty was looked down upon, severely. Such an act made her appear weak.

Standing quickly, the large guard named Gert backhanded her, sending her to the snowy ground again. He stood almost seven feet tall and carried a spiked baseball bat. It was common for each guard to take a turn at whacking the empty-handed returnee.

With a split lip, the woman rose to her feet and smiled. The sweet taste of her own blood filled her mouth as she sucked on the plump flesh. It made her hungry.

The tall guard grunted at her again.

The woman grunted back.

The communication between her people was simplistic, involving various sounds and gestures. Occasionally, words were used, their vocabulary growing.

She pointed down the hillside and indicated danger. The guards moved aside and let her pass.

She went up the stairs and into the cabin, passing numerous discarded bones of various sizes, all picked clean. The walls were damaged and marked up, the furniture stained and broken. Blood splashed the walls in streaks and handprints. She could still hear the foods' cries and it calmed her.

She made her way to the living room where the rest of her people, three females and five males in total, were hanging out. Fresh blood and bones littered the already saturated carpet. The leader, Ker, sat by himself, his axe by his side. Her people's skin was flawless, but the clothing was dirty, full of holes and smelled. It wasn't a bad odor but the smell of *her* people. The thing that greatly distinguished them from the food—besides how intact and unblemished their skin was.

The woman approached Ker and knelt before him. Eager-sounding grunts echoed around the room, quieting when she indicated that dangerous food was near the bottom of the mountain.

Ker stood and grabbed his axe, the blade decorated with crimson. He spoke, the words harsh and guttural, the pronunciations strange. The *new* people were beginning to speak some form of language.

Everyone stood at attention, picking up their weapons. Bats, pickaxes and machetes were raised high as howls cracked the air.

Ker batted his chest, giving the signal that the attack would happen now. The group's food source was almost gone. They would have to move, but before that time, they would eliminate a threat and eat at the same time.

With Ker spreading his arms wide, he gave the signal to head out. All would go on the assault and give their lives if necessary.

CHAPTER 16

Jack was shoveling a spoonful of beans into his mouth when a figure burst through the window next to the boarded up one. Glass shards flew like shrapnel, landing across the sofa where Maria and Henry were sitting.

Maria sprang forward, pulling Henry with her, the old man yelping as he crashed to the floor.

Jack was on his feet in half a second, sending his tray of food flying. With his .45 in hand, he raised the weapon to shoot when the figure disappeared behind the couch. A moment later, the intruder popped up and held a baseball bat above his head. Jack fired his gun, sending a bullet into the man's shoulder. The stranger groaned, but smiled and then leaped over the couch. Jack and Maria unloaded on the thing, its upper body becoming lodged with bullets. It staggered in place from the impacts, but then came forward. Finally, Jack shot it in its head and that's when the thing that looked human fell.

The window behind Jack exploded, the glass pieces cutting into his flesh like stinging bees. He spun around to see another figure land on the floor. Its clothes were ragged like the other's. It sprang at him as he fired his sidearm. The bullet hit the thing in the side of its neck. A moment later, it was on him—the creature faster than he'd expected.

It was obvious that the attackers weren't human. Not completely. They had to be infected, the bots keeping them alive like the undead. Or maybe they were fueled on meth or some other drug—*and* with the bots healing them. Keeping them alive despite the damage to vital organs. He thought of Henry's wife and what the old man had said. They had to be undead that had become human again.

As Jack fell to the floor from his attacker's weight and momentum, he made sure to hold onto his gun. Blood gushed from the human-like creature's throat where the bullet had torn out a hole. It had no effect on the thing as it clenched his throat and squeezed. He pressed the barrel of his gun against the thing's side and fired a few times before his attacker batted away the weapon. A normal human would've been dead or close to it by now. This thing showed no sign it was hurting and continued to choke him. He tried to pry its hands off him, but it was too strong. Its fingers were like steel.

Breathing was impossible.

Despite the fruitlessness of his efforts, he continued to try and loosen his attacker's grip. He wondered why Maria wasn't helping him—Zaun most likely still upstairs in the bathroom—and then he heard gunshots, but none hitting the thing on top of him. He knew then that more had entered from the other side of the room. It looked like he was on his own until Maria finished off her own attackers.

Jack's vision was fading, the outer edges growing black as if he was being sucked down a tunnel. There wasn't much time left. He wasn't sure he would die if he didn't get a breath soon. The bots might revive him. But then again, maybe they wouldn't. It couldn't end like this, not when he'd gotten so far. Found his sister's house with hope that she was alive.

The neck wound on Jack's combatant was hardly bleeding anymore and the hole was smaller. Jack saw malice in its eyes, the complete opposite of the undead. The bot-controlled corpses showed no sign of life, their eyes vacant. Blank. Both entities were killers, but these new creatures were worse, as hard as that was to imagine. The undead on steroids. He didn't understand why he himself wasn't stronger since the bots were in him too. Why had they worked better in the undead? In a few more moments, it wouldn't matter. Not to him.

Something metallic flashed above Jack. A line appeared across his attacker's neck and its eyes widened. Its head then fell onto his chest along with a downpour of blood. The pressure was off his throat and he choked in much needed air as the corpse's body pressed against him. A second later, the weight was off him. He cleared the blood from his eyes and saw Zaun standing over him holding out an arm.

Jack reached up and was helped to his feet. He thanked Zaun as he picked up his gun. Another body lay on the couch, its head containing two holes.

"I would have been here sooner," Zaun said, "but the toilet paper kept ripping."

"Yeah, right," Jack said.

"What the hell were those things?" Henry asked.

"Some kind of new . . ." Jack didn't have the words, then said, "Undead made human again."

"Explains the need for headshots," Maria said. "Well, not really, but at least we know how to kill them." Isn't that how they've been killing the undead this whole time? Headshots?

"They won't go down any other way it seems," Jack said. "And they heal quickly."

"Like we didn't have enough to worry about with slow-ass zombies," Zaun said.

Glass shattered from somewhere upstairs, causing everyone to flinch. A window had been broken.

"Shit, they're entering from upstairs," Zaun said, and went to leave the room when Maria stopped him.

"We should stay here," she said. "We don't know how many of them there are. They're obviously fearless, wild and quick, but not stupid. Why don't they all just come in through the door? Why from two sides? Then from upstairs? It's like they're testing us. Want us to lose our cool. Make us waste our time and energy worrying about all areas of the house. Divide us."

"We can't just let them in," Zaun said.

"It's our only option. We'll have a better chance at getting headshots with all of us firing from close range at wildly moving targets. We hold this room."

"And if an army gets in?"

"We head out one of these windows and hope we can make it to the snowmobiles."

The trio took up arms and readied themselves. The sofa was moved in front of the doorway, making it that much more difficult to get into the room. The desk was moved under the window on the left side of the den, the chunk of furniture making it so that they could escape on their own if need be.

As the group stood at the ready, crashing sounds erupted overhead and deep within the house. Glass broke. Objects were smashed. The ceiling above shook with the almost rhythmic stomping of a dance rehearsal group. Branches and rocks sailed through the windows at various times.

"It's like they're trying to frighten us into leaving," Henry said, keeping his M4 pointed at the doorway.

"It's a scare tactic," Maria said. "And a way to unravel their enemy."

"Why don't they just burn us out?" Henry asked.

When no one answered, Jack said, "I don't think they understand fire. They're like animals. Unfortunately, we don't know how long they'll be that way. They could quickly develop more cognitive ways of thinking."

A screeching wail sounded from down the hall as another zombie-turned-human charged the room. It was female and held a kitchen knife above her head, mouth and eyes wide. At the same time, two more intruders flew in through the windows at both ends of the den.

Maria fired her weapon at the one on her right. Bullets riddled its chest and face as it swung the club-like branch it was holding.

Jack kept his sights on the approaching female. Taking aim with his M4, he fired. The blonde hair on the right side of the thing's head fluttered with crimson. She kept coming, her wails louder. Jack fired again, not rushing his shot, but the woman ducked into the guest room across from where the laundry room was located. Damn it, he must have only grazed her.

On his right, he turned to see Zaun slice off the hand of another intruder who had been wielding a baseball bat, then plunge his blade into the thing's mouth, knocking out its front teeth. The sword's end exploded out of the back of its neck. It kept coming, the weapon disappearing into its mouth. The bot-infested thing swiped at Zaun's head. Zaun ducked and drove the blade toward the ceiling. His attacker froze, eyes bulging, and then collapsed to the ground as Zaun withdrew his sword.

"Never thought I'd say this, but I miss the undead," Zaun said.

"There's still at least one in the house," Jack said. "A female went into the guest room."

All eyes fell to the hallway.

More thudding and items getting smashed sounded from upstairs.

"How many fucking more are there?" Zaun asked.

"There's no way to know," Maria said. "Not unless we capture one and it can talk."

"Yeah, right," Zaun said.

"Only one way to find—" Maria began when the sound of a window breaking came from down the hall.

"The guest room," Jack said.

"Guess it's clear now," Zaun said,

Jack ground his teeth as he exhaled. This newest situation was frustrating. But at the same time, he was grateful to still be alive.

If the undead were changing, becoming humanly violent and able to think, then not only were he and the others in tremendous trouble, but so was the world.

***

The bot-infested woman stood outside the room she just escaped from. She had to smash out the window. Her skin was lined with cuts. They were minor and would heal in minutes. She had a decision to make: run or face her tribe. Life or death. Her duty was to enter the house and help frighten the food into leaving. Kill them if possible. Whether she lived or died didn't matter. The tribe and its leader were what mattered, not the lives of the singular.

But she was afraid of dying. Scared, like when the man with the sword killed the two stupid ones in front of her. And soon, there would be no tribe left. Not if they kept attacking this kind of food. Ker would never run though.

She shouldn't have reported on it. Half her tribe was gone. Slaughtered in moments. For the future, she would need to identify which food was safe and wouldn't fight back. Food she could handle.

Right now, she had more pressing matters. If Ker and the others found out she fled in cowardice, she'd be killed. It was time to go back inside or run away.

Not wanting to die, she took off through the tree line, across the neighbor's untouched snowy yard and kept running. She was scared to be alone and without a family, but the thought of dying was scarier.

CHAPTER 17

A number of hours passed without another attack, yet the grunting, howling, stomping and items getting smashed and splintered continued. The sounds came from inside the house as well as outside.

It was impossible to tell how many of the enemy was left, but the general consensus of the group was that the number was somewhere in the range of five to twelve. If it had been a larger group, they would have stormed the house in force.

"I can't take it anymore," Henry said. "I've got to see if my wife is all right." He headed toward the door. Maria jumped up and grabbed him by his shoulder. Henry shrugged her off, and it took her and Zaun to subdue him. For an elderly man, he was strong. Determined.

Maria spun him around so he faced her and said, "Look, your wife is either fine or already gone. If she's . . . alive, she'll need you to take care of her. If you get yourself killed, who's going to do that?"

The fight went out of Henry. His shoulders slumped. "You're right," he said.

Maria and Zaun released the old man, who walked slowly back to his position by the stove.

"Are you going to be okay?" Zaun asked.

Henry nodded. "I'll be fine."

Everyone went back to watching the windows and the hallway.

The noises of the enemy ceased when darkness fell, causing everyone to wonder if they had left. Like diurnal animals, darkness meant sleep.

The stove was ignited. With smashed out windows, the heaters weren't enough. The wind was entering in frigid gusts.

As time wore on and there was no sign of the attackers, Jack could see a weariness befalling the group. He was growing tired, too. Worn out from the tense situation and from having to remain standing.

"I think we should sleep," Maria said. "Take shifts of—" She paused, motioning for everyone to be quiet.

"What?" Henry asked.

The crisp sound of crunching snow and sobbing followed. A screeching cry split the air followed by a male voice calling for help.

Everyone looked at one another.

"Who the hell is that?" Zaun asked quietly.

"Please, help us," a female voice said.

"Is that for real or are they trying to trick us?" Zaun asked.

"No one moves," Maria said.

"Who are you?" Jack yelled.

"We were staying a couple miles away and were attacked, then brought here," the male voice said.

"Our whole group was killed," the female voice said. "And we were dragged off. We don't know what's going on or why we were brought here. But then we heard your voices."

That settled it. The enemy was able to reason to some kind of degree. The things understood people's emotions. It was incredible. Unless the enemy had been pretending to be animalistic. Maybe their attackers did know how to talk.

"What are your names?" Jack asked.

"Please, you have to help us," the male voice said. "These maniacs obviously want something from you."

"Names," Jack demanded.

"Eugene."

"I'm Stephanie."

"And the names of your captors?"

There was no response from either person. Then: "We don't know. They don't seem to talk."

Grunting.

Cries of pain.

"Please, help us," Eugene cried.

"We have to do something," Zaun said, sword in hand.

"We don't know what's really going on," Maria said.

"It could be a trap," Jack said. "Another way to get us outside."

More grunting followed by a howl and a sickening thud.

Stephanie screamed, and then said, "No, stop hurting him."

"How many of them are there?" Maria yelled. "We need to know."

"Five," Stephanie said.

"Do they understand you?"

"I don't think so."

Another cry of pain. Then a ripping sound and a male's wail that sent shivers down Jack's spine.

"They just tore his arm off," Stephanie cried. "His fucking arm!"

The sounds of fabric and flesh tearing, sinew being snapped apart like brittle twigs, filled the air. A pair of screaming voices accompanied the din of terror, but for only a moment. Then it was just the woman's voice.

"He's dead. He's . . . dead."

A boot flew through one of the den's windows. The foot and a small part of the leg were still inside it, the splintered tibia poking out like a crude spear tip.

"We need to help her," Zaun said, his stare intense. "There are only five of those things."

"Five that she saw," Maria said. "And it's dark. Getting headshots will be that much harder."

The woman screamed again. "Please, I don't want to die."

"We have to do something," Zaun said. "Go to the back door and take a look."

"He's right," Jack said. "We have to do that much. If shit looks bad, we fall back. Besides, I want to see what we're up against."

"Fine," Maria said. "But I'll go. Alone. The rest of you are staying here."

CHAPTER 18

Maria rolled her eyes and sucked in a breath as she made her way along the short hall, M4 in hand. The air was colder, bringing a rich chill to her bones. Reaching the corridor that branched off the main hallway, she allowed her eyes to adjust to the dark before peeking around the corner into the laundry room. A gust of wind blew past. The back door had been ripped off its hinges. Fragments of glass sparkled in the dim moonlight that shone through the doorway.

She stepped into the room. Avoiding the glass was going to be impossible. Each footstep was slow and gentle and she cringed every time a piece of glass let loose a shriek. The monsters outside would know she was there, that someone had left the den. It was what they wanted.

With a quickened pulse, she continued to take even breaths and moved forward. When she reached the open doorway, she had a partial view of the back and side yard. The snow was messed, trampled by numerous feet.

The girl barked a cry of pain, the sound off to the right and out of her view.

Swallowing, Maria poked her head around the door frame. With the moon's illumination, she saw the woman on her knees. Two of the four figures that were standing around her were holding her by her outstretched arms. Where was the fifth?

A grunt sounded and then the woman's right arm was jerked out. A popping sound echoed and her arm came free. Blood spewed as she screamed. The one who ripped off her arm peeled the fabric away and began eating the flesh. They were all looking at her.

Maria didn't react. They wanted her to see the woman die.

The woman continued to scream as her other arm was removed.

It took everything Maria had in her not to attack. But there was something she could do.

Raising her rifle, she took as best aim as possible and fired. The screaming woman's head burst apart. The figures howled. The headless corpse flopped to the ground as it was released. Their plan hadn't worked and they were pissed.

Maria surveyed the yard, looking for the fifth intruder. The couple had sounded so sure there were five.

Movement from above caught her attention. A fraction of a second later the fifth member of the party landed in front of her like some supervillain out of a comic book. It swatted the M4 out of her hands. The weapon clanged against the door frame. The tall figure swiped at Maria, but she managed to spring backward as its clawed hand whizzed past her nose. She landed on her back and drew her sidearm. Her attacker leaped like a panther.

She fired, pulling the trigger three times.

Brains exploded out the back of the thing's head before it landed on her, knocking the wind from her lungs. She couldn't call out and warn her friends that the enemy might be on their way inside.

Mustering her strength, she rolled the dead body off her and sucked in a breath. The air was fetid, like rotting meat. Her stomach churned. She remained on her back, gun pointed at the open doorway. If they were coming, she'd take out as many as she could.

"Maria?" It was Jack's voice. He was checking on her.

When nothing came through the door, she got to her feet. "I'm fine. Stay there." She needed her rifle, the M4 just outside the door. Moving forward, she approached the doorway and saw the maniacs charging. What had taken them so long to decide to do so was baffling, but there they were. They all held melee weapons, one with a leg in its hand.

She had a decision to make. Fight or retreat. A decision that could mean the difference between life and death for her and her friends. She could maybe take out one or two. Maybe. Then she'd be overrun. They would either kill her outright or use her as a hostage. Both results would be a detriment to the team.

Having made her decision, she grabbed the M4 and bolted back inside. As she ran down the hall to the den she alerted the others.

"How many are coming?" Jack asked.

"Four. One's dead." Maria took up position next to Henry.

The intruders roared and smashed the walls with their weapons as they raced down the hall. Maria took aim at the lead attacker and fired her rifle. The rest of the room followed suit, thunderous, ear-deafening gunshots shattering the air. The target's filthy shirt fluttered as bullets tore through it and into flesh. Its neck blew apart, sending gore against the wall, and then two bullets ripped through its skull. Its brains decorated the wall before its feet flew out from under it. Its brethren trampled it without slowing only to be met with more bullets.

They pushed forward, tossing the couch aside. Inside the room, they held their arms in front of their faces as if they were warding off spitballs. Another bot-thing fell as a bullet sent its brains across a female attacker's face. She shrieked as a bullet removed her nose, but she kept coming. She swung her machete two-handed at Jack like a wood-cutter splitting a log. He sidestepped out of the way, the blade missing him by an inch. She was quick and about to strike again when Maria aimed her gun and fired, sending a bullet into the attacker's eye socket, and then brain.

The remaining attacker dove at Zaun. Its body was riddled with holes, head streaked with blood where bullets had grazed it. Zaun stepped back, withdrew his sword and sliced outward, the pose Samurai-perfect. His attacker's head hit the floor a moment later.

The room fell silent.

"Is that all of them?" Henry asked. "I think my gun is empty."

"Yeah," Maria said, chest heaving.

"The woman?" Zaun asked.

Maria shook her head. "Dead."

"Damn," Zaun said, and kicked the headless corpse.

CHAPTER 19

After the attack, the group slept in shifts. Two were always on guard. But the rest of the night went without a problem. The bodies were placed outside the backdoor until morning when they were piled onto a sled and taken up the road and dumped. The house was cleaned up as best as possible, the windows boarded over and the back door reattached. Henry was going to stay at the house. He couldn't take the chance of his wife being shot by someone on the outside. Once she was normal again, he'd head over to the base. By then, the snow would be gone and he'd be okay and able to drive the Chevy Blazer.

Jack wasn't sure the man was making the correct decision, for no one knew what the future of the undead would be, but Henry told him he'd forgone leaving before when he had the chance and wasn't about to give up now. He'd probably die if he lost his wife anyway. Without her, and with his family gone, there'd be nothing to live for. He was old and had had a good life.

The weather was getting warmer, the air with less of a chill in it. The snow was melting from the rooftops and trees under the clear sky and the sun's bright rays. The white stuff was still too plentiful and deep to warrant ditching the snowmobiles for a car or SUV, but Jack couldn't wait for the day he'd be able to drive again. He was sick and tired of the cold and the snow and the darkness that came with winter.

They saw plenty of signs of life along their trek to the Air Force Base. Houses with operating chimneys, vehicle tracks, footprints, and a few people who had been just as curious as they were to see others. The snowmobiles were loud and had obviously alerted people to their presence. One young girl even waved at them.

These sights brought hope to Jack's heart and warmness to his soul. The land had seemed so ominous and hopeless, only filled with evildoers, but the people of Cliff House, Henry and these other normal survivors were good people. The world might have fallen, may have been changed forever, become tougher to live in, but people's spirits wouldn't be crushed or annihilated. It wasn't only the bad that survived.

As they approached the base, Henry's directions spot-on, a fighter jet flew overhead. The entrance was plowed, the asphalt beneath clearly revealed. There was no pile of corpses or bodies strewn about as he'd expected. But there was a ten-foot high wall. A number of armed guards were atop it, including a soldier manning a 50 caliber machine gun. All weapons were pointed at the new arrivals.

The snowmobiles stopped twenty feet from the entrance, engines killed. Jack removed his helmet and waited a moment to see if one of the soldiers would speak. When no one did, he said, " Hello," and gave a friendly wave. "We seek refuge."

"Are any of you infected?" one of the soldiers asked.

Jack was about to say no, then wondered if he should consider himself infected. Contagious even. Thinking about it, Zaun and Maria had gotten his blood all over themselves and neither showed signs of bot activity.

"No," he said, deciding it wisest.

"Leave the vehicles and stand on the pavement," the soldier said.

Jack and the others left their gear on the sleds and did as they were told.

"We're going to blast you with an EMP. Precautionary method of ensuring the base remains uninfected."

"They know about the bots," Zaun said softly.

"It would appear so," Jack said.

Maria shushed them and said, "Keep quiet, we don't know what they know. We act ignorant about everything until it's time not to."

Maria was right. If the soldiers knew about the bots, it could be because they have a science division set up and are studying them. They could possibly have been in league with Reynolds for all Jack knew. Part of that branch of the military.

Another soldier came into view and was holding a strange looking gun. It had a satellite dish-like end where normally the barrel would be. Curled wires ran from the stock's end to a large, square backpack. Another soldier appeared next to him holding an identical looking item. Both men pointed their weapons at Jack and the others.

Jack sucked in a frigid breath, pulse quickening. He had no idea what the EMP would do to him, to the bots coursing through his body. Yes, he was healed, but would his body break down if the bots were killed? Was his body reliant on the little things?

Suddenly, getting hit with an EMP seemed like a terrible idea. Maybe he should have asked if his sister was inside before agreeing to enter. Staring at the electrical weapons, he knew it was too late to change his mind now.

The EMP rifles jerked in the soldiers' arms as they were fired, the sound they emitted like a dull thud. Jack tensed. Breath held, he closed his eyes, but then opened them, not wanting to appear afraid. The military could not find out about his situation, about what he was. If they did, he'd become a human guinea pig.

"Leave your weapons with your vehicles," the soldier who'd been doing the talking said. "Take only personal items and food."

Jack couldn't believe he was still holding his breath and exhaled. He felt okay. Actually, he felt the same. Fine.

"We're not leaving our weapons here," Maria said.

"They'll be put in storage," the soldier said. "Should you want to leave, you'll have them back. Otherwise, you can hop back on your machines and head somewhere else."

Jack was so incredibly grateful he hadn't died, he spoke up and agreed for the others. They would all do as they were asked. Maria reiterated that she didn't like it but went along. Guns, Tasers, knives, grenades and Zaun's sword were all left with the snowmobiles. The front gate opened and three armed soldiers came to greet them. The trio were then escorted up a snow-cleared road.

"I'm looking for my sister," Jack said as they made their way toward a set of buildings. "Would someone know if she's here?"

"There's a list of all civilian occupants outside the mess hall," one of the soldiers said. "The reason it's there is exactly for a situation like yours. Lots of loved ones searching for one another."

"How many people are here?" Jack asked.

"The numbers vary. People are coming and going all the time. Flown out. Soldiers flown in. The military needs troops. This base does have a capacity limit, but it's a large one. If I had to guess, I'd say there are around 3,000 people on post."

Jack couldn't believe the number was so small.

"Don't look so grim," the soldier said. "We've probably had close to 20,000 people pass through here. That's not a huge number either, but when you see what's happened to the world, the numbers quite large."

They arrived at one of the housing units and were shown to their room, one they had to share with three other people. There was heat, electric and running water. Maria and Zaun showered. Unable to wait, Jack forewent getting clean and rushed over to the mess hall to view the civilian list. After searching through too numerous an amount of names to count, he found Sara's name. It wasn't crossed off and highlighted, meaning she was still on the base and had not been transferred.

Jack's heart swelled. She was alive and on the premises—at least if the board of names was up to date. Jack asked a man coming out of the mess hall if that was the case. The guy said it was as far as he was aware, that anyone who left the base was supposed to cross out their name and highlight it.

Jack checked the mess hall, but didn't find Sara. He asked a guard who told him to go to another building where an announcement was made asking Sara Warren to come to the mess hall.

Twenty minutes later, she arrived. Jack's eyes nearly leaped out of their sockets. She looked the same, if not a bit thinner. She met his gaze, their eyes locking. Disbelief masked her face, but quickly transformed into recognition. Her face brightened. "Jack?" she asked.

He nodded as tears fell from his cheeks. After all he'd been through, the doubt, the odds . . . He'd not only made it, but so had she.

"Am I dreaming?" she asked, approaching him slowly.

He hurried over to her and wrapped her up in a hug. They remained as one for some time, sharing tears and exchanging the love only family can share.

When they finally separated, they'd briefly chatted, asking one another how things were. Sara looked haggard, but who didn't. He asked about her husband, not wanting to say his name, and she shook her head. He'd gotten taken down by a group of undead.

They went back to Jack's room where he introduced Sara to Maria and Zaun. Pleasantries were exchanged and all three talked late into the night.

The next day, through the proper channels, Maria asked about getting to North Carolina. She tried to find out if her family was alive and where they might be, but the task was impossible. A week later, as sad as it was to see her go and after tearful goodbyes, she boarded a plane heading to Raleigh, North Carolina.

Jack, Sara and Zaun remained on the military base. Jack sliced his finger to test if the bots were still active, and when he didn't heal so quickly and wasn't ravished by hunger, knew the answer. He was normal again and glad to be so.

CHAPTER 20

The raggedy-clothed woman who had fled from her brethren changed her mind and made her way back to the house. She did not do this to rejoin her people, for they would surely kill her. She returned to see how they would fare against the enemy.

Sneaking up to the tree line that ran along the backyard, she found a thick, bushy pine tree and climbed it to the top. There she waited and watched as her people entered the house only to be slaughtered and carted off like garbage.

She had made the right decision not to stay with them.

What was her next move? she wondered.

With the enemy so powerful, she should leave. Should find food and a place to hole up in for a while. But something inside her told her to stay. A voice she was familiar with, the same voice that had previously told her to leave her people. Maybe it was curiosity or hope. She wasn't sure which. But then the enemy exited the house and departed the scene on their machines. Only the elderly man remained. He was old. Weak. She could see it in the way he walked. He would be no match for her.

She remained in the tree as the old man went back to his house. She would wait to see if the others returned, salivating at the chance of having a full meal to herself.

The next day, with hunger warming her gut, she climbed down from the pine convinced that the enemy was gone for good. She studied the house, noticing that all but two windows on the second floor had been covered, making it impossible to see inside. She wondered why all the windows hadn't been fortified, guessing that the two on the second floor were left open so the man could defend the house from there.

Observing the broken windows for a time, she saw no sign of the old man.

Ready to approach the house, she paused as the back door opened. The old man came forth, holding a weapon in his hands. It was a . . . She could not recall the name of the weapon. It was on the tip of her tongue like so many times before, as if from a dream or distant memory that eventually found its way to her. This had happened numerous times since she had been reborn. Despite the name of the weapon eluding her, she knew it could kill her. It made the weak and feeble old man much more formidable. Evened the odds. Once she killed him, she would take it for herself. Of course, she had no idea how such a thing worked, but she would figure it out.

The man made his way to the chest where the meat was kept. She could attack him now, but to do so could prove her death. The snow was loud when stepped on, crunchy. He would hear her approach from afar. She'd never reach him in time, not without getting severely hurt or killed. She would have to wait.

Gun. It was a gun, the word suddenly coming to her. *A shot-gun.*

The man took meat from the chest and returned to the house.

Upon his closing the door, she left the tree line and made her way to the back door. There, she stood. Listening, observing and waiting were important. Keys to survival. She had learned these things while most of her people had not. It was why she was still alive.

Having heard nothing, she tried the doorknob.

It turned.

Soon, she would have that meal she so desired.

***

Henry watched the door open. The woman with the raggedy clothes and perfect skin stood just outside the doorway. Her eyes widened as they fell to the shotgun pointing at her.

She hissed.

Henry pulled the weapon's trigger. The gun fired and the intruder's head blew apart, leaving a pulpy stump that spewed blood. The headless corpse fell back into the snow.

Henry let out a breath. "Didn't think I saw you hiding in the trees, did you?" He shook his head. "I may be old, honey, but I ain't no pussy and can protect myself just fine."

EPILOGUE

Jack, Sara and Zaun remained at Stewart Air Force Base where they took up jobs and joined the military. Jack became a guard on the wall that surrounded the base. Zaun and Sara joined the cooking staff, both loving to cook.

Along with Jack's, Maria's and Zaun's knowledge, the three explaining everything they had gone through, the powers that be gained valuable knowledge in the battle against the undead. The undead that were deemed the 'old' undead were shot on sight. The 'new' undead were the ones that had healed and appeared human. It turned out that was indeed the case. The bots continued to mutate. They were healing the newer undead. Turning them into vacant-minded people, their brains wiped like reformatted hard drives. Made anew.

Many of the new undead, now living people with bots in their system, were rounded up and hit with EMPs. A mass amount of education and reintroduction to society was going to have to take place. Cities were cleared of the old undead and made to house the new humans.

A small number of the undead-turned-living hadn't taken to becoming blank, docile beings that were open to society and its teachings. They became like wild animals, something off in their brains. A bad chemical imbalance. They became humanity's newest and biggest threat. There was nothing that could be done for them and they were shot on sight. Those that fled to the forests and mountains joined into groups and formed communities that were hunted and destroyed. It was impossible to eradicate them all. The Wild Ones, as they came known to be, were society's newest foes.

Jack didn't know what the future held. The planet and its human population would never be the same again. Maybe this time they could become better. Learn from the past. Whatever happened, he wasn't going to worry about it. He had his sister and best friend and planned on visiting Maria and her daughter very soon.

THE END

CHECK OUT OTHER GREAT ZOMBIE NOVELS

Z BURBIA
by Jake Bible

Whispering Pines is a classic, quiet, private American subdivision on the edge of Asheville, NC, set in the pristine Blue Ridge Mountains. Which is good since the zombie apocalypse has come to Western North Carolina and really put suburban living to the test!

Surrounded by a sea of the undead, the residents of Whispering Pines have adapted their bucolic life of block parties to scavenging parties, common area groundskeeping to immediate area warfare, neighborhood beautification to neighborhood fortification.

But, even in the best of times, suburban living has its ups and downs what with nosy neighbors, a strict Home Owners' Association, and a property management company that believes the words "strict interpretation" are holy words when applied to the HOA covenants. Now with the zombie apocalypse upon them even those innocuous, daily irritations quickly become dramatic struggles for personal identity, family security, and straight up survival.

ZOMBIE RULES
by David Achord

Zach Gunderson's life sucked and then the zombie apocalypse began.

Rick, an aging Vietnam veteran, alcoholic, and prepper, convinces Zach that the apocalypse is on the horizon. The two of them take refuge at a remote farm. As the zombie plague rages, they face a terrifying fight for survival.

They soon learn however that the walking dead are not the only monsters.

CHECK OUT OTHER GREAT ZOMBIE NOVELS

900 MILES
by S. Johnathan Davis

John is a killer, but that wasn't his day job before the Apocalypse.

In a harrowing 900 mile race against time to get to his wife just as the dead begin to rise, John, a business man trapped in New York, soon learns that the zombies are the least of his worries, as he sees first-hand the horror of what man is capable of with no rules, no consequences and death at every turn.

Teaming up with an ex-army pilot named Kyle, they escape New York only to stumble across a man who says that he has the key to a rumored underground stronghold called Avalon..... Will they find safety? Will they make it to Johns wife before it's too late?

Get ready to follow John and Kyle in this fast paced thriller that mixes zombie horror with gladiator style arena action!

WHITE FLAG OF THE DEAD
by Joseph Talluto

Millions died when the Enillo Virus swept the earth. Millions more were lost when the victims of the plague refused to stay dead, instead rising to slaughter and feed on those left alive. For survivors like John Talon and his son Jake, they are faced with a choice: Do they submit to the dead, raising the white flag of surrender? Or do they find the will to fight, to try and hang on to the last shreds or humanity?

CHECK OUT OTHER GREAT ZOMBIE NOVELS

VACCINATION
by Phillip Tomasso

What if the H7N9 vaccination wasn't just a preventative measure against swine flu?

It seemed like the flu came out of nowhere and yet, in no time at all the government manufactured a vaccination. Were lab workers diligent, or could the virus itself have been man-made? Chase McKinney works as a dispatcher at 9-1-1. Taking emergency calls, it becomes immediately obvious that the entire city is infected with the walking dead. His first goal is to reach and save his two children.

Could the walls built by the U.S.A. to keep out illegal aliens, and the fact the Mexican government could not afford to vaccinate their citizens against the flu, make the southern border the only plausible destination for safety?

ZOMBIE, INC
by Chris Dougherty

"WELCOME! To Zombie, Inc. The United Five State Republic's leading manufacturer of zombie defense systems! In business since 2027, Zombie, Inc. puts YOU first. YOUR safety is our MAIN GOAL! Our many home defense options - from Ze Fence® to Ze Popper® to Ze Shed® - fit every need and every budget. Use Scan Code "TELL ME MORE!" for your FREE, in-home*, no obligation consultation! *Schedule your appointment with the confidence that you will NEVER HAVE TO LEAVE YOUR HOME! It isn't safe out there and we know it better than most! Our sales staff is FULLY TRAINED to handle any and all adversarial encounters with the living and the undead". Twenty-five years after the deadly plague, the United Five State Republic's most successful company, Zombie, Inc., is in trouble. Will a simple case of dwindling supply and lessening demand be the end of them or will Zombie, Inc. find a way, however unpalatable, to survive?